Death

Elizabeth Oakey

Paperback ISBN 978 0 6455925 1 1

Ebook ISBN 978 0 6455925 0 4

Prologue

At something of a loose end after the "trials and tribulations" of my honeymoon, the Godfrey Ball was as good a distraction as any, although I dare say I don't need to tell that it all got a bit out of hand.

I hope you won't regard this entire book as some kind of job interview, which is how it subsequently felt, and I trust that I haven't given the impression that the Cotswolds is a dangerous place. I'll be the first to admit that Ampney Tet has had more than its fair share of unfortunate incidents of late, but I'm confident that it hasn't had any more garrottings, poisonings or stabbings, than Creech St. Michael, Whimple, Nether Wallop or Plumpton have. (Make of that what you will.)

Kind regards,
Georgiana Mortimer

P.S. I hope you will also notice that my reintroduction into polite society has been successful. And if you happen to be on intimate terms with either of the editors of *Domestic Bliss*, I would be most grateful if you would mention it.

One

Freedom! I caught sight of my uncle's Bentley, and was about to skip over the road towards it, when I remembered the telegram. It was from Aunt Bathsheba. A guard had handed it over as I was taking my first step *outside* – and it said simply, "LAY LOW".

Slowing to a sedate walk, I wondered just how much fuss my aunt thought I could drum up crossing Camden Road, although I suppose my being picked up from His Majesty's Prison Holloway, was the salient point. Innocent as I was, the fact remained that I was emerging from jail.

As I opened the car door (far quicker than waiting for Baxter the chauffeur to do it for me) I was met with the attentions of a leaping, licking, yelping dog, doing her best to make up for all the attention my months in jail had denied her. Darling Crumpet! Our reunion was frenzied and a little wild, but she eventually allowed me to slide into the back seat and settle myself.

Glancing over at Baxter, I noticed that he appeared to have grown a luxuriant ginger moustache since I'd last seen him, and it was only as I looked closer that I realised it was held in place with hooks around his ears. It looked like he wasn't sure he wanted to be seen out with me, a feeling that was forced home when Baxter spoke.

'Mornin' madam, it's a cold mornin' so it is, and there's a blanket there in the back if that's what you're wanting,' he said, in an accent that may or may not have been an attempt at an Irish brogue, but I couldn't blame Baxter for that. My life had changed dramatically since the last time he'd driven me anywhere. I shivered.

Little Crummy had shredded the silk stockings I was wearing, and I'd never thought I'd miss the thick woollen ones we were issued with in prison, but I buttoned up my coat and wished I'd had a hat. The clothes I was dressed in, were an outfit I'd last worn to the funeral of the husband whose murder I had been wrongly imprisoned for, and the lack of hat and the soft, luxurious fabrics made me feel a little half-dressed, after months of regulation grey linen.

And my mood was further deflated, when Baxter informed me that we were off to my uncle's estate in the Cotswolds, rather than my aunt's smart terrace house in Pimlico. So, what London couldn't handle, country folk could, apparently. It had been a long, tiring few months and, keen as I was to see the outside world, Crumpet and I fell asleep almost as soon as Baxter left the city's outskirts.

It was the middle of the afternoon and despite the chill in the air, the low sun cast a golden glow on the limestone of the grand house in the distance, which sat on the top of a hill at the end of a long, gravel drive. We have arrived at Ampney Tet, my Uncle

Lawrence's estate, nestled in the fair, green bosom of the English countryside. After months in Holloway, the scene before me seemed unreal; I wound down the window for a breath of bracing air, all the better to comprehend my new surroundings, and allow Crumpet to enjoy the ride. The air was really very bracing indeed, so I rearranged the blanket over my knees, and only then noticed the coat my aunt had left in the back of the car; an opera cloak. The same velvet cloak I had worn on Christmas Eve – my wedding day, a couple of months earlier.

I had married Edward Mortimer – or rather, the man I knew as "Edward Mortimer". We had left our wedding reception in London, and almost as soon as we'd arrived at the cottage we were to stay in, he had been killed. And since then, I had been locked up in HMP Holloway awaiting trial for his murder, while my aunt and her team of romance writers investigated on my behalf, and managed to get me out. And here I was, free as a bird; a widowed bird who'd spent her honeymoon incarcerated, and was now free, but to do what exactly?

As the car rolled up to the front steps, Auntie Bathsheba pirouetted down them.

'Come in, come in, come in, Georgiana, my dear. We have mulled wine and mince pies to warm you up.'

'But it's March!' I said, as I alighted from the car, and with Crumpet at my heel, walked up Ampney's grand steps.

'Yes, I know, but your Christmas wasn't what it might have been, and there was some of the mixture left. And anyway, who doesn't love a mince pie? Baxter? Bring up the luggage, will you? Oh! No need, perhaps?' She glanced down at the paper-bag I held – which contained my copy of *The Count of Monte Cristo*.

Before going inside, into the warm, I paused on the top step, to take in the rolling hills, leafy clumps of trees, the sound of distant birdsong and the lively smell. It was all very familiar, and for a moment, my time in prison felt like a nightmare from which I had just awoken. I just hoped that society at large felt the same way.

'Your Uncle Lawrence is at his club. He thought you might need a breather, and so it is just the three of us,' said my aunt, as Maude took the cape from my shoulders.

Maude is my aunt's maid, and although some people of my aunt's station might have been inclined, in those circumstances, to count my aunt and myself as *two*, Maude would never stand for it.

'Good to see you back, Georgiana,' she said. 'And not before time. The library's fire is lit, and there's liver for dinner.'

'Do we have to?' asked my aunt.

'That's what Cookie's got in, so unless someone else wants to do the cooking, liver it is.'

'I'm sure I said something along the lines of a Christmas dinner,' said Bathsheba, 'But that evidently fell on deaf ears. Cook is something of a traditionalist. She only agreed to make those mince pies because the mixture's seven years old and Maude insisted. Really, we should be grateful she hasn't prepared bread and water, given your recent trials.'

It had been a meagre couple of months as far as food was concerned – there had been plenty of liver served at the prison on a regular basis, but I said, 'Liver will be fine', hoping that the disappointment wasn't too evident.

'That's the spirit!' said my aunt. 'Speaking of which?'

'Mulled wine coming up, and sherry for those who want to drink something nice,' muttered Maude over her shoulder as she walked out of the room. 'And Crumpet? I've seen what you've done to your mistress's stockings, and I'd like a word.' I was surprised to see the little dog reluctantly follow the maid along the hallway, and off to the kitchen.

'Maude has taken the dog's training in hand,' said my aunt. 'I think you'll be quite impressed, although there were tears.'

'Crumpet didn't bite, did she?'

'It's Maude who bites,' said my aunt.

Given my recent stretch in prison, my aunt said I was well within my rights to spend a week or so relaxing while I got used to wearing my own clothes, not having to watch my back and being able to have a cup of tea, a biscuit and a lemon sherbet **whenever I wanted one**. And mindful of my recent imprisonment, I returned to the little cottage I often stayed in whilst on the estate. It was less fuss for everyone, according to my aunt, but I also wondered whether it was a convenient place for me and Crummy to stay while people came and went – with no questions to be asked about my change in marital status and my time away. In fact, I couldn't have been more wrong. I was at the centre of a whorl of organisation and upheaval and I quickly realised why I had been brought to the estate, rather than being returned to town. It hadn't been because Sheba thought I could do with some country air after my time "inside", nor was it because she thought I should have some calm and time away from London society. In fact, quite the opposite.

We were in Ampney Tet because the Godfrey Ball was coming up.

No wonder Bathsheba had been so incredibly relieved that I was out. Not only was I not committed to a lifetime in prison – or worse, of course – I was home in time to help set up the house for the biggest social occasion of the year. It was an occasion that took up a great deal of organising, and my aunt would have had little time left to spend in my defence, had I not been released from prison when I was. (But let's not think about that, shall we?)

Two

Every year that the ball was held, my aunt bemoaned the fact that she hadn't kept notes from the last time, and I couldn't recall how many years ago that had been. Which led me to wonder why Bathsheba had decided to hold a ball this year? There had been a very real chance I wasn't going to be able to attend, one way or another.

'Don't look at me like that, Georgiana. It was your cousin, Gerald, who decided on the date, and he made that decision before you were married. Something to do with the jazz band he wanted to hire. He said there was a long waiting list for them, and that they were the "bee's knees". Of course, if you had been in prison –'

'– or worse!' I said.

'– if you had been *in prison*,' she continued, 'It would have been a far more muted affair. And as it is, you're here to help out – which is wonderful!'

I had no doubt at all that my aunt's maid, Maude, knew exactly what was supposed to happen for the ball to be a success, but that she wasn't interested in adding to her work load. I didn't blame her, but wondered whether she was right about that. When my aunt became agitated, she also became more demanding, and Maude shouldered most of that burden; although with me at the estate the load might be shared...

And why hold a ball anyway? As you may or may not have already guessed, my aunt and uncle are not awash with funds, despite their "honourable" status (Lawrence is the second son of a baron). And although they like to convey the casual insouciance of their class, they are like a duck on a pond; appearing to glide serenely on the surface, while their legs flap, flail and thrash under the waves for all they're worth. The ball is a chance to spread the word about my aunt's publishing house and names are added to their mailing list. And my uncle's contacts within Westminster – and the printing and paper world are deepened, and hopefully built on.

Not for them a life of sheep herding – or watching sheep being herded.

My first night of freedom, Maude and I walked over the lawns to the little cottage, and opened the door – or rather, I tried to open the door. For a moment, I was reminded of the bedroom door that wouldn't open in Mean Withering – and my husband's body behind it. I took a deep breath and tried again, only to find that the little home was stacked full of crates of champagne, piles of laundered napkins and polished punch bowls. We pushed until it opened and, with Crumpet firmly held, wondered how the footman had managed to get these items in in the first place. There was no question of me getting through to the bedroom, and when Maude saw the state of the cottage, she told me to stay in the nursery in the main house until the party was over.

The next two days were spent sorting out table settings, ordering and arranging flowers, ensuring the grounds were looking as good as they could – and making last minute adjustments to the menu, our outfits, the table linen and the limited number of cushions we had available for the older guests to sit on. All in all, it was harder work than Holloway.

Given that it was the end of March it was the first ball – and one of the last hunting meets – of the season. Family were invited, friends were invited, locals and Londoners were invited. The great, the good, the fun, the useful, the lovely, the good-at-cards, the bad-at-cards and the mediocre-but-known-them-for-ages-and-too-much-trouble-NOT-to-invite were invited. It was going to be a big night – and a pretty impressive morning. Breakfast was going to have to be spectacular too.

'Oy, Georgie! What are you going to wear?' said a voice from under the stairs.

It was the first time I'd seen Jack since the doomed wedding reception, and she was a sight for sore eyes, even if she was wearing a pair of dungarees that looked like they belonged to the gardener.

'Jack! You're in your writing gear, I see?'

'So many hours at a typewriter, one has to be comfortable,' she said, although she didn't exactly smell like she'd been worrying a Remington's keys. Had she been cutting grass?

'In answer to your question about what I'm going to wear,' I said, 'I have absolutely no idea. I came out of the clink with nothing, and was brought straight here. It's widow's weeds or grey linen. Take your pick.'

'Your aunt wants to see you!' It was Maude. 'Upstairs in her room, quick as you like.'

'On my way!' I bellowed back. 'And may I ask what you're going to wear, Jack?'

'The usual,' she said. 'Tie and tails. They're in a paper bag in the kitchen.' And when she saw the look on my face, she told me that she'd folded them!

'Look forward to seeing you later, Jack – and at this rate, I'll be borrowing your dungarees.' I bounded up the stairs to my aunt's boudoir. It was a large, sunny, pink and green bedroom decorated with golden-framed mirror and embroidered silks, and it was exactly as you'd expect. And my aunt was sitting at her dressing table, resplendent in baby-blue satin and marabou feathers.

'I heard mention of your outfit for the evening a –'

'How –'

'–and I haven't forgotten you, Georgiana, not in the least. I asked my three daughters-in-law to bring a selection of gowns over and they've been very obliging. Of course, there's no question of you wearing Cecily's – she's far too broad about the beam, and you're far too tall to fit into anything that Alexandra has to offer, but you should fit into something of Louisa's.'

Opening the wardrobe was a heady experience. There was a rush of perfume, sparkle and colour – so many colours. Smooth golden silks, joyful cherry-red beads, emerald-green lace, sumptuous sage velvet, gleaming black satin and brilliant silver sequins. It was all so luscious and lovely, that I forgot to breathe for a moment. I was brought back to earth with a bump, when Maude said, 'We haven't got all day. It's nine hours until kick off. There are three hundred napkins waiting downstairs, and they won't fold themselves.'

'I'm afraid Maude does have a point,' said my aunt. 'We have had something of a domestic crisis ever since that incident with the swans, and we're a little low on womanpower, so, if you wouldn't mind...' Maude was just leaving the room, when my aunt called after her 'And we are not making animals this year. Too fiddly. It isn't the thing, Maude. Napkins folded in half and absolutely no flamingos!' There was no reply.

Rifling through the dresses on offer, I opted for a navy-blue silk with silver beads. It was exquisite – until my aunt reminded me that it was what Louisa had worn last year. Ah. The teal silk with the handkerchief hem? Oh, that was her New Year's Eve get-up at the ball on the next estate along. I see. And the black velvet? Worn at a murder mystery weekend in January... In the end, I opted for a gold-fringed satin which was really very lovely, but... no, really, it was lovely.

HUNDREDS of napkins later, we were allowed a reprieve from manual labour, and ordered to bed. 'A two-hour nap,' said my aunt. 'And then up at four to bathe, get dressed, have a cheese and pickle sandwich and a little snifter before the hordes arrive!' With aching legs and weary fingers, I traipsed up to the nursery and curled up in a cot.

Three

Ampney is the largest party venue for three counties, but my aunt and uncle haven't the staff or the coal money to keep the entire house open, the whole year round. Indeed, if it weren't for this ball (and the occasional do held by friends whose own quarters aren't up to scratch) half of its rooms would never be seen; hidden behind closed doors and under dust sheets.

After a wake-up call from Crumpet, I quickly dressed, had my hair arranged and sent the little dog to the scullery, where Cook had promised her a bone. Then, I rushed downstairs to join my aunt and her Girls – Jack, Lettice and Bettina – the writers she employed, who were in the library quaffing sherry and having a quick bite to eat before the hordes arrived.

And just half an hour after that, the house was heaving with guests.

The collective volume of the Bright Young Things was a little on the ear-tingling side, but they were having a fabulous time. Only the married invitees bothered with the Jacobean ballroom which was far too drab for a proper party, with all its dark, heavy carving, no – the conservatory was the place-to-be and that was where everyone had enjoyed their first glass of champagne, and where the younger set remained once the band began to play. It was ideally suited to the summer, of course, but warm enough when it was full of people – and it was wonderfully lavish. Designed by a Victorian with a penchant for Louis XVI, it offered layer upon layer of glass and crystal. Indeed, its chandeliers were so generously mirrored and monstrous that, dangling overhead and tinkling in time with the music, I feared that the crystals were about ready to drop.

I had been married for half a day and I was now very much single, so after waltzing with the mature marrieds in the ballroom, I did the Charleston with the shingled singles in the conservatory.

Where to go next? I sashayed my way through the throng, and stood at the conservatory doors. They opened onto the grand steps that led down to the South Parterre and, given the faint nip in the air, I was surprised to see the terrace and lawn littered with almost as many lovelies as the dance-floor inside. The girls were beautifully wrapped in velvet and silk, and the boys didn't look too shabby either, although it had got to that stage of the evening when bow ties, natty little boleros and ropes of pearls and beads were going by the wayside, hung over cast iron seats and stone planters – and even crunching underfoot.

Cheeks were flushed with booze and there was much braying, snorting, sniggering and chortling, cocktails were flowing and everyone was a picture. Dizzy was sitting on the lap of Binky, I don't know who Emera was with but it wasn't Gerry, and Daisy was supposed to be with Johnny but was actually with his twin brother Jimmy, and they must have known, but neither of them was letting on.

I pulled my stole around my shoulders and turned, only to bump into my aunt, who was dancing to her own sweet tune, and gazing up at the conservatory's elaborate ceiling which was adorned with fluffy clouds and plump, rose-cheeked cherubim.

'Georgie, my darling! Are you having a lovely time?' It was my aunt, who was being steadied by Maude with one hand, and holding a tray of champagne coupes with the other. Both women were glassy-eyed, and when Maude tilted the tray in my direction, I took a glass – if only to balance her load.

'I am having a lovely time, Auntie Sheba,' I told her. I wasn't sure that I was, really, but it would only have been mean to have said otherwise. 'It's just... it's just that it's a long way from Holloway,' I said, and then a bread roll sailed overhead, and I thought perhaps it wasn't so far after all.

'Such a shame we couldn't have got Patrick Balfour over from the Daily Sketch, or Lockhart from the Standard. Someone to mark the occasion, and put us in the papers. Still... perhaps just as well, given the circumstances.' She patted my hand and, fixing me with a (slightly swaying) gimlet eye, my aunt told me that a couple more coupes of champagne would sort me out. I decided she might be right about that, but before I set to the serious work of partying, I mentioned that I'd been looking for Lettice.

'Last time I saw her, she was in the billiards room with the Kiss & Swoon fan club enjoying a little chat with Mr Cullimore, an elderly suitor. He's a rum old fellow, and she really ought to watch herself, but she thinks she's doing him a favour, and he thinks the same about her, so they're quite well matched really. Apart from the sixty-year age difference.'

'She isn't!'

'Don't worry about Lettice, she's far too quick for him. And as pure as the driven snow unless Mr Stone is anywhere nearby, and then she turns a bit soppy.'

'I had noticed...'

'And before you ask, Stone's son isn't here either,' she said, referring to Benjamin Stone, the young man who'd been my solicitor during my recent imprisonment. Or at least, I'd thought he was my solicitor – he was in fact a student and, in the words of his father, I'd been the source of some marvellous experience. (Well – thank you very much!)

I decided to catch up with Lettice, and taking a sip of my aunt's champagne, I left with a smile and a shimmy, and after much meandering, I managed to walk into the hallway, where I found Bettina, sitting on the steps of the grand staircase. She was holding court; surrounded by a group of wide-eyed women, and it was hard to tell whether they were appalled or enthralled by her stories, but I had no doubt she would get readers out of it. And Lettice? Bettina pointed me in the direction of the billiard room; she was still there.

It was large compared to most of the billiard rooms I'd seen, and with the table in its middle, the outer edges of the room were raised on a dais, all the better for the people on the chairs at its edge to see how the game progressed, but how the people sitting at the sides could see through the cigar smoke, I couldn't say. If I hadn't been able to hear the knock of the billiard balls, the men at the table could have been playing cribbage.

I peered through the smoke, and finally found Lettice, sitting next to a small, very elderly man, who was gazing at her fondly while stroking her hand. She, however, was looking the other way, holding a cheese puff in her free hand and in deep conversation with a group of half a dozen women my aunt's age – presumably the fan club my aunt had referred to.

As one of the women walked past to say something to Jack, I noticed the fond gaze of Old Cullimore follow her too, although he didn't for a moment stop stroking Lettice's hand as he did so. And while he remained silent and watching, the women to Lettice's right seemed oblivious to their surroundings – so involved were they in their conversation, and all of them with at least one glass to hand, if not one in each – and passing them on.

There was little room for the footmen, so the room's occupants were taking the trays at the door and handing out the glasses and nibbles themselves, and roaring with laughter as they did so. Their heads were bowed together in conversation, and now and again one of them would laugh uproariously. Just for a moment I was reminded of the witches from Macbeth, and I wondered what they were cooking up in the swirling mist of mugginess.

As I looked about me, it seemed that everyone had a slightly Bacchanalian glint in their eye – if not a leer or a sneer. The everyday had gone away; the evening had a timeless quality about it and we were wrapped in a runaway world of pleasure, and excess. There would be tears, and I also wondered whether perhaps I'd had a little too much to drink.

The men playing billiards were being watched by Jack who was, in theory, doing the scores, although how she was managing to keep an eye on the cannons and pot-shots while regaling a companion with the story of a cowgirl she'd encountered at a rodeo, I couldn't imagine. (Had she even been to America, let alone the Wild West?)

The younger of the two players, whose turn it was, was concentrating hard on a shot, while the older, larger man barked instructions. The shot went wide, and the "instructor" began a lengthy explanation about what had gone wrong, that the younger man evidently wasn't enjoying. His mind on other things, he kept glancing at the doorway, presumably looking for someone to whisk him away, onto the dance floor.

When the older man took his shot, it also went wide, and he rubbed his palms on his trousers, muttering about the warmth of the room. When the younger man suggested he chalk his hands as well as his cue, he pretended not to hear and demanded Jack tell him the score.

A waiter managed to complete a circuit of the room with a tray full of a variety of drinks, and as he was about to leave, his tray was emptied by the "fan club". He left with the tray tucked under his arm, and I followed him out, back to the conservatory.

The Jazz Misfits – the band for whom the entire bash had been organised so far in advance, were playing a soft, slow piece that reminded me how alone I was in this crowd of people. I finished my drink and decided a proper dose of fresh air was in order.

Four

I marched out the door and twirled down the conservatory steps, down to the edge of the formal lawn. The stars shone bright and there were plenty of invitations to share a drink, but I was drawn towards the shadows. I needed to be alone for a while. I veered off to the right, skirted round the pavilion and sat on those steps for a moment, drinking in the beautiful pastoral view: completely contrived of course but stunning, even in the moonlight.

When I'd had my fill, I got up to carry on round but not before I caught sight of Roger Elton, strolling around, and if there was one man on the entire planet I wasn't in the mood for, it was Roger, besides which I couldn't see why he was doing the whole solitude thing. It didn't suit him. He is the least mysterious man I've ever come across. He carries himself with an extreme confidence built almost solely on the strength of his Aquiline nose, which, while very fine, is no substitute for a personality. He thinks he's a tricycle at Christmas, when the truth is he's the bruised tangerine at the bottom of the stocking... or the lone nut.

I slid over the stone balustrade, dashed round a couple of corners and found myself in the coal yard. I could hear him calling my name, and I had to put my hand over my mouth to stop laughing, which only made me more hysterical. As I rested for a moment in the shadows I heard a whinny, which I took as an invitation to visit the stables and check on Madrigal Girl – one of my favourites. I wandered through the dark in her direction.

The musty smell of the animals was comforting after the heady scents indoors and I stopped and rested my forehead on the cool stone of the stable archway for a moment's rest. I opened the door and walked around for a while, looking over the gates at the horses in their stalls, until I found the beautiful chestnut. Madrigal Girl was fifteen hands high, elegant and even-tempered. Too much so, according to the head of the hunt who had implied she'd never be really great, a remark that had struck me as a bit silly and suggested that the woman had never fallen from a horse, which seemed unlikely.

Always very grateful for a carrot, I took one from a bag in the tack room, and lent over her door. Madrigal Girl nuzzled my hand and I was just stroking her muzzle when, out of the corner of my eye, I saw the broad, beautiful shoulders of Firth, an old flame of mine. He was always good for a smooch and we'd been friends of a sort for a while, and he was standing at the far end with his back to me, leaning against the gatepost. The moon must have clouded over because the stable became a series of nebulous shapes, Firth amongst them.

I decided to surprise him and sidled towards his long, lithe body holding my pearls taut so that they wouldn't give me away. I reached out, stroking his shoulder and felt him stiffen, so I moved my hands upwards and ruffled his hair at which point he quietly gasped. I threw my arms around his and held him tight, and it was only as I was toying with one of his buttons that I realised his shirt was linen, and he spoke... in a deep, confident bass that wasn't familiar. 'Hallo?'

My fingers froze and I jumped back, into the shadows. 'Firth?'

'Ummm, no.'

'You're not Firth!'

'Nope. Never said I was.'

'But you could have said something!'

'To be fair, I just did.'

'You could have said something a bit earlier!'

'Well, it all seemed to happen quite quickly, what with the hugging and the... caressing.'

'That isn't funny!'

'No, it isn't. I was standing here, minding my own business when you came over and molested me.'

'I did not molest you. I was just....'

'You were just?'

'Ummm –'

'Do this often? Walk up to a strange man and start something?'

'But I ...' His deep voice was smooth and annoying, and he was *quite* infuriating, and still unknown to me, standing under the gloomy eaves. Try as I might, I couldn't conjure up a suitably cutting response, I didn't have much of a defence, and was forced to take an abrupt step forward into the deeper shadows that surrounded him as the clouds shifted and a shaft of light shone down, threatening to expose me. If I was embarrassed by my lack of *bon mot* I oughtn't to have been because the strange man carried on anyway.

'You could have the decency to tell me who you are! Or is this it? You're just going to walk off and that's the end of it?'

'Well, I don't know what you expect!'

'After what you've just done, dinner at the very least. I would suggest the pictures but you obviously can't be trusted in the dark.'

Oh! I'm afraid the champagne had rather got the best of me, and for want of a sparkling riposte I reached round and pinched his bottom. He promptly gave mine a curt smack; I slapped his hand and he slapped mine! We were standing face to face in the pitch darkness and I was still no wiser as to who he was or what he looked like, but really this was too much!

'What did you do that for?!' I hissed.

'I might ask you the same thing. And it's your turn... what's it to be next? Ping-pong paddles at dawn?'

'You are an infuriating man!'

'And you ought to be careful who you fondle in the dark!'

'Fondle?! I did not!' It was obviously a lie, but again, I was at a loss for words and thought it better to retreat at speed. So, I stomped off, still able to make out remnants of more of his tomfoolery as I went.

'Take care won't you,' he called after me. 'You should be careful though, there are some shady characters about.'

Once I was far enough away and could no longer hear his infernal chatter, I glanced back, curious to see who I'd just, well, molested, but even though the clouds had cleared he remained in the shadows, as did I.

Turning the corner, I saw the distant warm light of the party and heard gay laughter; my heart dropped and I slowed down a little, anxious to allow my cheeks to pale before being seen in the light. And then what happened? I bumped into Roger again. Hell's bells! He sidled up to me and I decided a turn of speed was in order. Catching his foot as he stepped towards me,

I angled my shoulder into his and pushed; he went a pearler and I resolutely carried on. Why on earth hadn't I thought of that before? And that was when I realised that I would never have known how to do that if I hadn't been to prison and been taught *suffrajitsu* by Phyllida – and I wondered what the women were doing now? It had been half past eleven, last time I'd seen a timepiece, so they were all safely tucked up in bed – with the possible exception of Marjorie, who may have been troubling a keyhole with her set of lockpicks.

I trudged back inside, caught my reflection in one of the mirrors and went to my room to reapply my lipstick and wash off some of my rouge. My cheeks were quite red enough as it was. I also had to change one of my stockings, which had a great long run in it. As I loosened my garter and rolled the silk down, my head swam and I decided a cup of tea or a glass of milk was in order, if I was to survive until breakfast. I dabbed scent on my wrists and was about to add some to my neck, when I heard a scream.

The kind of party it was, the odd scream wasn't unusual, but this scream was odd – so odd that even the music had ground to a halt. I ran downstairs, and it was apparent from everyone's turn of head, that whatever had happened was serious, and it had happened in the ballroom. And it was even more apparent, when the words, "HE'S DEAD!" rang out from that direction.

Five

In fact, it wasn't the ballroom, it was the billiard room beyond that the scream had come from, although half the folks who'd been in the bigger room, were now trying to fit into the much smaller one. And chief amongst them was my aunt, who looked rather cross – in contrast with the rest of the crowd, who looked shocked. Lettice was weeping, and staring appalled at her hand which was still being held by the elderly gentleman by her side, and he was sitting very still. Very still indeed. Ah. So, he was the problem.

A waiter walked past with a tray of cups of tea, and I took the opportunity to lighten his load, and have a sip – hoping that it might take the edge off some of that booze. With cup in hand, I pushed my way through the throng towards Aunt Bathsheba, but was beaten to it by a man I recognised as the local doctor.

'Ferguson!' said my aunt. 'You've come at just the right time, and you are the only person who can help poor Mr Cullimore. TOO MUCH CROWDING. OFF YOU GO TO THE DANCE FLOOR! EVERYONE SHOULD BE WALTZING. NO EXCEPTIONS!' she roared.

The ring of people began to disperse, some of them saying things like, "I hope he's all right, is he asleep?", and others saying things like, "Death on a dance floor I could understand, but sitting watching billiards?".

Uncle Lawrence joined me, and he had evidently just come from the buffet table, because he was holding an oyster. 'Well, that's two ways of looking at it,' he said.

When I'd poked my head in the billiard room earlier, it had been mostly full of women, along with the two men playing billiards, and those same people were still there, but they had been joined by dozens of others – and me, of course.

I saw Maude pass Lettice a cup of tea, her hand was free now, but she remained in her seat, fixedly looking away from the dead man sitting next to her, muttering something about having thought he was having a nap. Bettina led her out of the room, in search of a quiet corner.

And with the space around the gentleman cleared, one of the footmen arrived with a trolley, which he manoeuvred around the back of the chair. He managed to hoick the poor man up and take him (still seated) into another room, while the elder of the billiards players barked instructions at him and walked close behind. They were followed by Dr Ferguson, my aunt, my uncle, me – and the other, younger player, whose face was drawn. Unfortunately, it was the library to which the "casualty" had been taken, and it was the library to which Bettina had taken Lettice a minute earlier. The woman was quite distraught as we all entered, and my quick-witted aunt flicked a curtain over the dead man's ruddy face, and ordered the two writers to leave. 'Go and get some trifle, both of you. Off to the kitchen! Now... where were we?'

The doctor pointedly removed the curtain from Mr Cullimore, and began to examine the small, frail man. It should have been clear to anyone that he was dead – the colour of his face, the slightly strangulated expression he wore – none of it was good, but the doctor had to go through the motions.

'And what time is the gentleman believed to have died?' he asked.

My aunt looked none the wiser.

'If Lettice's scream was anything to go by, that was about seven minutes ago,' I said.

'That makes it about a quarter to midnight,' he said, looking at the clock on the chimneypiece. I'll add that to my notes. And in the meantime, we shall wait for an ambulance to arrive and take Mr Cullimore away from the party.'

'That would be just as well,' said my aunt, 'It's terribly inconsid–'

'– terribly *unfortunate* that this has happened,' I said, correctly my aunt's lapse in vocabulary.

'You realise you're only wearing one stocking, Georgiana,' she said, 'Or is this a new thing the young people are doing?' and with that, she left me and the doctor to deal with Old Mr Cullimore.

Most of the guests continued in a devil-may-care manner, many of whom had been given rather more to talk about than they'd banked on. And a small number were openly sad and grieving, including the young billiards player who, it turned out, was the dead man's great-grandson, Peter.

According to Jack, he was rather talented with a cue and would have played better if his father – the older man – hadn't spent each game telling him what to do next. 'He won a nice pocketful of notes before his father insisted on giving him a lesson. And before old Cullimore went off like he did…' she said, 'Quite the windfall, and – hullo, who's this?'

A young woman entered looking stricken, tears rolling down her face, her sunset-red hair was tied back under a small cap, although some curls had come free, and there was a leaf tucked behind her ear – from an orange tree. She was Mr Cullimore's nurse, if the colour and cotton of her dress was anything to go by, although the length of its hem was surely not regulation for a uniform, and it was a little tighter than would have been comfortable.

'Why's he covered up like that? What's wrong with Mr Cullimore?' she asked. (My aunt had covered him in the curtain again.) Jack pulled the young woman aside and told her what had happened – and she fainted as she heard the news. A flock of men rushed forward to catch her, but Jack was too quick for them, although many pairs of willing hands carried her over to the chaise longue to recover.

Meanwhile, Baxter and the doctor waited for an ambulance to arrive. And the jazz band played on.

By the time breakfast rolled around, six hours later, Mr Cullimore was all but forgotten, as a small number remained behind, to take advantage of devilled kidneys, curry, kedgeree, kippers, porridge, sausages, gammon, bacon and left-over trifle. It was a fine feast to bid farewell to the stolid few, and send them on their way – whether that was off to the stables, or to bed.

Three hours later – and after less than half an hour's sleep, I was amongst the welcome committee assigned by my aunt, to greet the hunt. The riders arrived at the door, and were bid a good morning by my bleary-eyed Uncle Lawrence, with a tray of sherries and port. I stood in the cold, giving out sausage rolls, and shivering, and through the morning mist, I noticed a rider I recognised. I congratulated Jack on being well enough to get up so early, and noticed the horse she was going to ride. Oh! It was Madrigal Girl!

In all the fuss and bother about Mr Cullimore, I'd quite forgotten my little *contretemps* with Roger – not to mention my moonlit meeting with the mystery man in the stables. I hurried back inside, and took to my bed for a couple of hours more kip.

Six

Lunch was all but forgotten, and dinner was a subdued affair for everyone except my aunt, who decided it was the best ball they'd ever held.

'Are you sure about that?' I asked.

'Did you see the looks on the youngsters' faces? And that band! You know, I think I quite like a bit of jazz. Might have to have them over for my birthday.'

'And Mr Cullimore?'

'Mr Who? Oh! Ah, yes, Mr Cullimore. Yes, that was unfortunate.'

'Still, we all have to go some time,' said my uncle.

'But not at my ball!' said my aunt. 'I won't use the word *inconsiderate*, I know it wasn't his choice to go when he did, but... well, I can't think of a better word. That's all I'll say.'

'I've no idea who he was,' I said, 'Apart from being old school.'

'Oh, he would have loved to have heard you say that,' said Lawrence. 'Old? Certainly, but old school? No. In fact, he came from nothing very much, as far as I can tell.'

'I had no idea,' said my aunt, and written all over her face was the question why they had ever entertained him, especially given his *behaviour*.

'Cullimore was a self-made man,' said Uncle Lawrence, stirring an alka seltzer and soda – and lightly flinching at the din it was making. 'Started off as a newspaper delivery boy in Worcester, I believe, and worked his way up and was a member of the Paternoster Club and a farmer and – oh, all sorts of things. He had a great deal of land, many times what we have.'

'Well...' said my aunt. 'His newspaper I was NOT impressed by, and they allow all sorts at that printing press club of yours, although I will concede that his asparagus was another matter entirely.'

'Asparagus?' said Lettice, 'Ugh! Can't stand the stuff.'

'You certainly made enough of a fuss about it when it was served at the ball,' remarked Bettina.

'I was offered it TWICE!'

'Served with a Hollandaise sauce, it can't be beaten,' said Uncle Lawrence.

'You're absolutely right, darling, but sadly no more asparagus for you,' said my aunt. 'Doctor's orders! It causes gout!'

'Rubbish!' said my uncle.

'The chicken and asparagus vol-au-vents we served yesterday, were thanks to the late Mr Cullimore's crop,' said Maude, stepping in to quell rising tensions. 'The season begins on Saint George's Day, but he gave us special access to the first crop. I'm not sure how we'll manage next year...'

'I was right, you see,' said my aunt. 'Inconsiderate!'

Old Cullimore had been the oldest man at the ball by a long chalk – and arguably the richest. But when Dr Ferguson popped in for a visit the following morning, we learned that Mr Cullimore hadn't died in an inconsiderate manner at all.

He had been *murdered* in an inconsiderate manner, which was something quite different.

'Well, the pathology has report come back,' said the doctor, taking his seat. 'In fact, I was rather surprised they tested for anything at all given the man's age, and the levels of excitement that evening, but the ambulance driver didn't feel he should have been looking quite as *pink* as he did.'

'I see,' said my aunt, who still looked cross about it.

'Given his advanced age and, apart from a bruise on his foot and a scraped elbow, Cullimore was in very good condition,' said the doctor. 'Well... aside from his having passed away, obviously.'

'Is there any question that it was deliberate?' I asked, although the doctor was undoubtedly right about Cullimore's colour when he'd been taken away.

'Oh Georgie, really!' said my aunt. 'It could have been a bad oyster. Not one of ours, obviously, but something he'd had at home before he left.'

'Ah yes, about that...' said the doctor, at which point we heard a knock on the door. 'The police should be around about now.'

Our local bobby was Detective Inspector Harrow, an old acquaintance of my aunt and uncle's, and if he hadn't been visiting his mother in Bournemouth for the weekend, he would almost certainly have attended the Godfrey Ball in a private capacity.

'Afternoon all.' The voice wasn't Harrow's, but it was one I recognised.

'Good morni-afternoon,' said my uncle. 'Routledge isn't it?' There was an awkward moment that passed once we'd all decided that there would be no mention of the last time we had met. Inspector Routledge had been in charge of the investigation of my husband's murder, as a result of which I had been sent to jail.

Maude was good enough to give the man a mulled wine (what was the time?) and my uncle went on to ask if he had come about the Cullimore business.

'I have indeed,' he said, taking a long sip from his goblet – long enough that he'd surely drained the thing. And sure enough, a little nod from Auntie Bathsheba was sufficient for Maude to pour the inspector a second cup, whether he wanted it or not. (I think we were all feeling a little nervy at this change in our circumstances.)

'So, you think the man was poisoned?' I asked, and the officer abruptly stopped drinking. 'You see, Dr Ferguson indicated that he was a bit pink.' I pointed at the doctor in the corner.

'Ah, I see.' He put the cup down. 'Yes, Miss-Mrs Mortimer...' My married name hung in the air, and I gave the man a brief nod to indicate that I was happy with the title. 'The toxicology report has come back, Mrs Mortimer, and I'm not entirely sure the doctor should have been quite as free with his words, as he was.'

There was a harrumph from the corner, and the doctor suggested that if it had been poison, there was always a chance traces of it remained on cups, glasses and cutlery, in which case it was his duty to tell the homeowner; at which point all of us put our drinks down, with the exception of my aunt.

'Come, come,' she said, 'Everything has been cleaned, and none of us is looking at all green around the gills, are we?'

'But the doctor did say "pink", and isn't that a sign of cyanide poisoning?' I asked.

'GEORGIANA! Shush now!' My aunt took a deep breath and composed herself, before turning to the doctor. 'Thank you, gentlemen, for bringing the matter to light. In a lesser-run establishment with questionable levels of hygiene that might have been information worth having, isn't that so, Maude?'

The maid nodded and took the doctor's half-drunk cup of tea – and his untouched piece of Victoria sponge – away, and the rest of us drank on (in solidarity, you understand. There really was no question of Maude's house being unclean).

The rest of the afternoon, young constables came and went, wiping, sniffing and peering; investigating Mr Cullimore's death in one way or another.

Hiding in a corner of the library with a small, snuffly dog and a book (no, not one of my aunt's publications or, indeed, my uncle's) I was found by Bathsheba, who arrived with Maude in tow – and she came bearing a pot of Oolong and a plate of shortbread.

'I'm seeking sanctuary here, with you,' she said, 'It has been *quite* an afternoon, and Lettice... well.' My aunt lowered herself gracefully onto the chaise-longue, and reached for her cup.

'Yes, I wanted to ask you about that. When the inspector told us we had to stay put in the county, and all that silliness about us all being suspects, Lettice said, "Not again!" What did she mean, *again*?'

'Caught up in the heat of the moment,' said my aunt, with a vague wave of her hand, before rapidly turning the topic of conversation to Crumpet. 'Such a good little dog, aren't you? I'm sure Cookie will have something suitable if you ask nicely.'

The little dog understood and left us. My aunt took a sip of her tea. 'One thing I hadn't realised about my mother-in-law, was her special interest in poisons, and it certainly explains her attitude to the Harvest Festival. It turns out most of her walled garden is toxic in one way or another, and I'm very glad we got on as well as we did. Which isn't to say *well*, but presumably well enough for me not to have merited anything home grown.'

'What did she have in there?'

'I've no idea. They've taken samples of everything for testing. Rather a charming bouquet, but I'm hopeful they won't find anything too irksome. It's not that I like having a poisonous garden, but it is pretty and it would be a lot of trouble to have the gardener dig it up and start again. And it's not like Gilgamesh and Xerxes are going to succumb to any of it, all the way out here.'

My aunt's Persian cats live in the townhouse in Pimlico. They were not likely to lick anything in a wicked walled garden located in the middle of the countryside, although I would have to keep my eye on Crumpet.

I nibbled a shortbread and heard a voice ring out from the billiard room. It was Jack. 'I don't know what you THINK this is, but it's French chalk, I tell you!' I finished my biscuit and skipped over to see her explaining to a young policeman that he was going to ruin the billiard table's baize if he kept on rubbing it like he was. There were traces of white powder on it, but Jack was adamant that it was billiard chalk.

'Billiard chalk is *blue*,' said the young man – quite correctly in my opinion.

'Billiard chalk is *often* blue,' said Jack, 'But the player in question brought his own cue and his own chalk, and his chalk was from Paris where the chalk is white, not blue! *BLANCHE PAS*

BLEUE!' and with that statement, she bent down, took a great sniff of the patch of dust he was talking about, and marched off. A sneeze rang out as she disappeared from sight. 'IT'S JUST CHALK!' she yelled.

I wasn't sure what Jack had managed to prove, but she had certainly made a spectacle of herself.

SEVEN

As I mentioned, we had all been asked to stay in the county while enquiries were ongoing – which is something Uncle Lawrence would ordinarily have been happy to do, had we all left for London, as we usually did. My uncle is a man who enjoys company on his own terms, and when he grumbled about it, a young constable (who evidently had no idea *who* my uncle was) cheerfully told him that the death had occurred in his home, which put him at the top of the list of suspects. Old Inspector Harrow certainly wouldn't have put it like that – and I doubted that Routledge would either, but my uncle's face was a picture.

Still distinctly disgruntled, he joined the rest of us in the library, which was empty of police staff as it had already been swept for fingerprints. My aunt airily told the young constables covering the space that they could expect at least 150 people's worth of fingers.

'187 more than that, madam,' said Maude, 'If you include the staff and caterers – who are also people. Not to mention the policemen who marched in and touched stuff before they'd even started. And if you times all of them by the number of fingers they have, that'll take it to a tidy 3,367 prints.'

'Surely not!'

'Mr Jenkins is missing a few.'

'He'll have even fewer fingers by the time he manages to get this ink off,' said my aunt. 'I can't see mine ever being pink again!'

'I don't know why they're bothering to take the fingerprints of anyone who isn't a woman,' said Uncle Lawrence, with uncharacteristic vexation, rubbing at his inky hands. My uncle is generally the calmest, most thoughtful person in any room, but when he's had enough (or someone steps on his gout-ridden toe) he turns, not for long, but he turns. 'Poison is very much a tool of the fairer sex,' he went on.

'Oh, yes, why's that?' asked my aunt.

Lawrence obviously hadn't caught the tone of her voice, and he carried on, despite a long, loud sigh from Jack.

'They haven't got the strength for any of that other business,' he said.

'Not got the strength to pull a trigger?' asked Bettina, lightly.

'It's not just the trigger,' said my uncle. 'You've got to point the bally thing. Aim, you know.'

'You're confident that if I were to fish a revolver out of my desk drawer right now, and point it at you, I'd miss?' said my aunt, eyes blazing.

'I'd be right as nine pence!' he said, taking a sip from his tea.

'You might be right about that,' said Maude. 'After all, your mother planted that garden of poison out there. And one of the women downstairs undoubtedly made that cup of tea you're drinking...'

My uncle harrumphed – and put his cup down.

With the ball well and truly over, Crumpet and I were allowed to move into the cottage I usually frequented and, with my distinct lack of luggage, I sauntered over and opened the door. It was a simple two-up two-down – nothing like the cottage in which I'd spent Christmas Eve with Edward. The floor was swept, the woodwork was freshly painted, the fireplace gleamed and the welcome was warm.

I filled the kettle and put it on for my first pot of tea in my new, albeit temporary home, and I sat at the kitchen table. I couldn't help wondering whether what my uncle said was true, and about the previous twenty-four hours. If Old Cullimore had been poisoned, there was someone out there – possibly a woman – who was happy to murder, and it piqued my interest.

Crumpet's interest, meanwhile, had been piqued by a deer she could see out of the window, and I rushed to slam the door to stop her from running off in pursuit. 'Oh no you don't! Go on, find a warm corner and have a lie down, you've had plenty of walkies today!' I immediately regretted having said the "w" word, of course and, in the end, I had to resort to giving her the half a sausage I'd had tucked in my sleeve for a training session later in the day, with Maude in charge.

While Crumpet happily lay in front of the fire, I went upstairs, and inspected my accommodation. The wrought iron bed was tucked in the corner, next to the window, which was open and rattling in the wind, all the better to air the place. I leaned over and shut it, and realised that what I'd taken for a patchwork quilt was in fact a neat arrangement of clothes – Louisa's cast-offs – rather chic items suitable for daywear.

I had been released from Holloway Prison with the clothes I'd been incarcerated in, and when Baxter had picked me up, we hadn't stopped at my sad little flat in Clapham, and I still had none of my own clothes, with the exception of some undergarments I'd picked up in Cirencester. (I have my limits, and so does Louisa.) I held up a stylish little blue wool dress and opened the wardrobe door – to find it full to the brim with boxes and bags. The topmost one had a label on it, which said, "To the Newly-Weds! With best wishes, from Auntie Agatha, Johnny and Albert x". Oh.

All of the boxes were wedding gifts in honour of a marriage that had lasted less than a day, and that, in the end, had been founded on a lie. Was I supposed to return them?

I popped downstairs to make my tea, where I found a card propped up against the tea caddy. 'Too late now. No point in giving them back. Enjoy! Love N.', and I recalled my aunt receiving visitors after I'd returned to London from my honeymoon in Mean Withering. It seemed that all the parcels were mine, and I traipsed back upstairs, cup in hand, downcast – until I saw the names on the boxes. A silver coffee pot and cutlery from Liberty's, matching alarm clocks and a salt and pepper set from Asprey's, table linen and towels from Selfridges, and a tea set from Royal Worcester; this last gift, given with love from my aunt and uncle. Oh, and a bottle of tequila from Mexico – care of my mother.

It was all beautiful, but was it mine? Sort of. But did I deserve it? I gave it some thought and, by the time I'd finished my cup of tea – and reflected on my disastrous one-day long marriage and months spent in prison – I had come to the conclusion that perhaps I did.

And I expect you're wondering where that beautiful car has gone – the Sunbeam Tourer that my uncle bought for me from my late husband's first wife.

Thanks to my uncle's legal representative, the elder Mr Stone, it was to be released from a court lock-up in London, very soon. The documentation was due to come through any day now, and then I would get my hands on that lovely, leather steering wheel. A little part of me was afraid that it would always be Edward's car; while he had been alive, I had only ever been the passenger, and the only time I'd actually driven it, I had served prison time as a result.

But I was almost sure that as soon as I sat in it, with Crumpet at my side, a roaring ride into the countryside would brush the cobwebs out of my hair, and it would feel entirely different.

(And with all that regimental silver Edward had stolen, cleared from the car's undercarriage, I was sure it would handle much better too.)

EIGHT

'Bettina has lost her latest book!' announced my aunt, marching into the cottage, closely followed by Maude, who was carrying a pot of tea and quarter of a fruit cake. (It was five minutes to eleven and the perfect time for a little something.) Aunt Sheba took a seat and waited for me to take mine. (I'd been about to have a cycle ride around the estate as the sun was unexpectedly shining, but the bicycle and the lack of rain would have to wait.)

'What was she reading?' I asked. I'd picked up an abandoned paperback earlier, and was afraid it might have been hers.

'It isn't what Bettina's reading that's the problem,' said my aunt. 'It is what she has just written!'

Bettina was a bit of a mystery – although that wasn't what she wrote. Her series, as far as I knew, was called "Purple Velvet" and was nothing like Lettice's Regency romances, or Jack's cowboy tales – although as I say, I had no real idea of any of them. Well-dressed, possibly a little too well-dressed by British standards, I guessed Bettina was English but may have been wrong about that. Had she, perhaps spent a long time overseas? Her consonants were clipped, but too much so? All in all, Bettina was more than your average woman – especially around Ampney, and I couldn't help wondering what time she got up in the morning. Her stockings were always perfectly straight, and shown off to perfection by the slit up the side of her skirt, which was just a little higher than necessary. Her hair was beautifully lustrous and straight, and her body was a temple – or the site of some kind of cult, although her waistline was, well, a little old-fashioned. Naturally nipped-in? Hard to say, but for a certain kind of man, she was, well, perfect. She made no mention of a husband or particular companion, although she seemed to know a lot of men and there was nothing shy about her. I gathered from my aunt, that her writing was always delivered on time, in stark contrast with the other two, and that it required little in the way of editing (also in stark contrast with the other two). She was an impressive horsewoman, oh – and she had once mentioned, in casual conversation, that she was good at knots.

I also guessed that Bettina had friends who were less salubrious than one might have imagined of a romance writer, but what did I know? One of her pals had got me out of a tight corner in jail, and if it hadn't been for that particular woman's help, I'm not sure I'd be sitting here writing this now.

Aunt Sheba told me that she had arranged a meeting with Bettina in the billiard room after lunch, to discuss the loss of her latest creation, and that my presence would be welcome. She had a task for me.

I spent the rest of the morning riding with Jack. She was on Madrigal Girl, and I rode Cheery Bob. We cantered along the country lanes, trotted through the fields and tried a couple of jumps. It had been a long time since I'd done any riding, and it felt good to be back in the saddle. Late for lunch, we were granted a sausage sandwich each by Maude, and told to get dressed before "The Meeting".

I returned to the cottage, primped my hair, changed out of my plus-fours and gave Crumpet some water, before running back to the house. When I arrived, Bettina was waiting for me, looking like I'd never seen her before. Her hair was a bird's nest of anxiety, her stockings had twisted, and she was biting her nails – or, one of them, at least. She looked like she'd either just got out of bed, or never been to sleep – and I should point out at this point, that if I ever look half as pulled together on my best day, as Bettina did on her worst, I would be delighted.

'I understand you've lost a manuscript,' I said. 'Can you tell me what it looks like?'

'Paper. Lots of words on it,' she replied, striding up and down the room, taking a long puff from a long cigarette in a very long holder. 'Sorry, Georgie. That was uncalled for. It's a novella. Fifty pages, hand-written in indigo ink with a fine nib, enclosed in a red manilla folder. My initials are embossed on the front.'

'Which are...?'

'B. A. S. Bettina Ariadne Savage in case you're wondering.' She angrily stubbed out her cigarette and marched out of the room.

I joined in the hunt for the manuscript, and even opened a few files that were blue and yellow, but it was hard to know what all the fuss was about, until I spoke with Jack about it.

Apparently, it had been written in an experimental style that Bettina had tried once before, and I wondered what that meant? Iambic pentameter? First person? Second person? No person? But when Jack quietly mentioned that Bettina had suggested that there were certain likenesses among the characters she'd written about that might be just a little too obvious – a little too close to the bone – I began to see what the problem might be. I had an idea that Bettina wrote slightly racier stories than either Jack or Lettice (well, obviously!) but I got the feeling that, if Bettina were worried enough to actually show it, then those stories must be on the steamy side. And if she'd written about easily recognisable people...

'Our subscribers wouldn't mind, of course,' said Jack, 'But if it were to get into the wrong hands, it might make things rather awkward.' She said it in a way that suggested that would be rather entertaining, and in truth, she didn't look in the least bit concerned. Lettice was a different matter entirely, and she was rushing around, this way and that, looking under cushions, behind books, around doors and under carpets. It was exhausting just watching her.

I asked all the usual questions. Where did you see it last? Who knew that you'd written it? And got vague answers. It seemed that she'd made the very un-Bettina-like mistake of using one of her embossed folders to contain the contact details for the jazz band, and the string quartet that played at the ball. Oh dear.

And finally, almost afraid to ask, I enquired as to the manuscript's whereabouts when the police had been over, to examine the billiard room after the death of Mr Cullimore.

Auntie Bathsheba looked at Bettina and Bettina looked back. 'Let us assume it isn't in the hands of the local constabulary,' said my aunt, 'Aside from anything else, I think they would have been over to have a little chat with us about it by now...'

Neither woman was prepared to discuss who the local persons might be who could possibly be identified in the script, and as far as I could tell, there was no question of blackmail – yet.

'And Georgie, seeing as you're the only one here who doesn't have any deadlines due,' said my aunt, with a raised eyebrow at her writers, 'I shall make it your mission to find this manuscript. A job, if you will. Ask around and see what's become of it. Oh, and if you could also find out whoever thinks it's acceptable to poison people at my social gatherings, that would be most helpful. The police have been sniffing around the walled garden again, although I'm fairly sure it doesn't include cyanide.'

With nothing better to do, and curious to know more, I nodded – and carried on looking for the manuscript.

It hadn't been found in the house, there were no red-tinged ashes in the fireplace, and no demands for money or arrest warrants issued.

It was a mystery.

And Mr Cullimore's murderer? That was a mystery with no arrest warrants issued either.

Nine

Bathsheba announced at breakfast the next day that the writers were returning to town; she didn't want their output to become 'rural'. And my reminder that they weren't supposed to leave the county was waved away, impatiently.

'What time are they leaving?' I asked.

'Before lunch, I'm happy to say. You know what they're like, they're eating us out of house and home,' she said, taking another kipper.

It was imperative that I had as much information about the night of the ball as possible, before they left, so I shovelled in the rest of my kedgeree, and ran out the room to locate the three ladies before they headed back to London.

I found Lettice in the orangery, sniffing delicate fruit trees. I didn't blame her, it was the warmest part of the house and, when she told me that the others were upstairs getting their things together, I told her to meet me in the library in five minutes.

After bumping into Maude and asking for a fresh pot of tea, I ran up and down corridors, poking my head into rooms I hadn't investigated since I was a child, and I eventually found Bettina in one of them, a second-tier bedroom by the looks of it; nice but old bedding, a northerly aspect – and I wouldn't want to try out the mattress.

I told her about the meeting I was holding, and that I was looking for Jack.

'She's probably having a romp in the stables, or the hayloft,' she said, with an impenetrable expression. Was Bettina making fun of me or Jack – or was it worth looking into? I poked my head into the next five bedrooms, just to be sure.

When I got to the stables, they were empty of all human life, so I gave the horses a carrot each – to stay in their good books – and then followed the sound of banging.

Jack was in the garage – a small ivy-clad building also known as the coach house – and she had a hammer in one hand and a piece of wood in the other.

'Hullo, what are you up to?' I asked.

'I'm already packed,' she said, 'And I had a bit of time, and I was thinking about Tony. He has one of those fiddly, modern cues –'

'You're talking about the billiard cue that belongs to Anthony Cullimore – the son of the old man who died?' I said, taking a closer look at the stick in her hand.

'His grandson, actually, but yes. Well, his is Italian-made, and rather fancy. Inlaid and all that business. It comes in pieces. Tony twists the bits of it together and carries it around in a case. You'd never know what was in there. He's very keen on the game and has always brought his own chalk and his own cue, and he's always fiddling with it, adding attachments...'

I wasn't very good at billiards, but I had played the game at Ampney and could only assume Anthony had taken a dislike to the cues that were available to play with. One of them appeared to have been designed for my aunt (or a seven-year-old child), and the other was most likely made with Gary Cooper (or his taller brother) in mind, and felt like there was a lead weight embedded in the end of it. I didn't blame the man for bringing his own.

'I was waiting to play billiards with Tony when Old Cullimore fell ill,' said Jack.

'Were you there all evening?'

'Most of it. Tony and Pete, his son, were in and out all evening long, and when one of them was out, I played billiards with the other one,' said Jack. 'Or I was out and about, you know – checking out the dance floor, picking up a pastry or hunting down a glass of champers – which was just as well, because the waiters had stopped bringing drinks in to us. Too crowded, too smoky and too much going on. They were just leaving great trays at the door.'

Great trays of drinks that anyone could have tampered with.

'Anyhow, I just wanted to see if I could improve on the equipment we have.' (Looking at what Jack had done to the cue in her hand, my immediate answer was 'No'. Jack's ways with a typewriter were legendary. Loose key or blurred letters? Not a problem. Type bars jamming or ribbon sticking? Fixed in a jiffy. But carpentry was evidently not a skill of hers – the long cue had become one very short cue and a stick.)

'What did you notice while you were playing – about Old Cullimore, I mean?'

'For most of the evening, he was sandwiched between Lettice and his great-grandson, Pete,' she said.

'And was he drinking anything?'

'There was plenty going around – trays of champagne, beer, wine, gin, cocoa, tea, and even water at one point. I didn't see what he was drinking, but he was telling some fairly fruity stories about the folks at the village Rotary Club. And he spilled a drink too.'

'Was he a bit tipsy?'

'Well, he had a cue dropped on his foot, so he chucked Tony's ale back at him and it was only Lettice's intervention that stopped him from storming off. Although he was very old, so it might not have been as dramatic as he'd have liked.'

It sounded like Mr Cullimore had enjoyed a variety of drinks, whilst telling stories about local businessmen that Jack said were "fruity". I was beginning to think that the question wasn't how many suspects there were, but who could safely be excluded from enquiries.

'And if you're wondering who poisoned the old man, I should mention that we were all drinking everything. Old Cullimore took from the same trays as the rest of us. He didn't ask for anything special at all, apart from the sachet of *cachet faivre* from his nurse.'

'He had a headache?'

'Actually, Cullimore said he wanted to make sure he didn't have one.'

Jack further revealed that the grandson, Anthony, had been playing billiards the entire time, and that he had been nowhere near his dead grandfather. And as far as she could recall he hadn't given the Elder Cullimore a drink, passed him any food, or handled the man's glass.

Satisfied with the questions I'd asked Jack, I returned to the library, where I met Lettice and Bettina. They had poured my tea for me, and it was lukewarm and had been left too long to steep in the pot, but still...

Both of them confirmed what Jack had said about the huge number and variety of drinks and nibbles being passed around the billiard room, and I couldn't help thinking that, given the amount they'd consumed, it was a miracle anyone had remembered anything – and a miracle that Old Cullimore was the only person who'd succumbed that night.

Maude came in and topped up the pot with some hot water, and helped herself to a cup at the same time. In addition to knowing that the funeral would happen later in the week, when Cullimore's body was released, she also told us that the great-grandson had been overwhelmed with grief at Mr Cullimore's passing – and had taken to his bed for a couple of days. (Maude knew his butler.) But the young man's father, the grandson, was another matter altogether. He had been upset, of course, but he'd popped up to London for another shindig as soon as the hunt was over, and (according to Maude – and in the words of the postmistress) Anthony had only *deigned* to return to Ampney Tet to assist in arranging the funeral, when he'd received a call from the vicar.

My enquiries over with, the ladies gathered their cases, coats and – in Jack's case, duffel bag, together and Baxter took them to the station for the 10.30 from Kemble to Paddington.

My aunt was somewhat surprised when she got a call, that afternoon, to pick them up again; they had returned to the countryside. They told her that there was a problem with the Pimlico house gutters, and water was running down one of the interior walls. Oh, and a window had cracked, so the place was freezing – even colder than Ampney.

No, they couldn't be expected to create literature under those conditions. Yes, they had contacted Lawrence about it and he had said that some man at the Paternoster Club would sort it out. And, yes. Xerxes and Gilgamesh were having a whale of a time at Mrs Moore's house round the corner – and enjoying trout twice a day.

Ten

While we waited for Baxter to return with the writers, I decided to ask my aunt some questions that had been nagging me. 'What was the name of the young woman who was Mr Cullimore's nurse?'

'I have no idea what her name was,' she said, 'And no idea why he had a nurse, he was as fit as a flea!'

'I agree entirely,' said Maude, clearing the plates. 'Why would a man of 102 want a twenty-year-old lovely with legs all the way up to her armpits and a come-hither look hanging around at his beck and call. No idea at all.'

Hm, she had a point. 'Although whatever-her-name-was, she was very affected by the news,' I said. 'And yet...'

It was Maude who said, what I could not. 'He was a hundred and two! How long did she expect to nurse him? And what kind of a uniform was that she had on?'

I had to agree, but she must have done some nursing at some stage in the evening, because I had noticed a couple of fresh dots of blood on her uniform.

'Old Cullimore used to employ nurses long-term,' said Maude, 'With all the fuss that goes with that, but in recent times he'd had quite a string of them until that redhead came along.

But if you want to know anything, Mrs Burrows who runs the library might –'

'We do not speak of the library,' said my aunt.

'As I said, the LIBRARIAN, runs a little local agency on the side and she almost certainly found him his helpers. And Mrs Burrows, can be located at the Dirigeon-Cullimore Trust Free Library just off the high street.'

The Dirigeons own a neighbouring estate, and they are a source of great annoyance to my aunt for reasons too numerous to go into – and Mr Cullimore's land was a little farther along – and another source of annoyance. And my aunt's mood was not helped, when Maude left the room muttering something along the lines of, 'If you'd thought to build a library, with or without the help of a neighbour, you'd have your name on it, and I wouldn't be consorting with "the enemy" for the sort of books I like to read!'

I decided to go in search of Mrs Burrows, so, putting my walking shoes on, I called for Crumpet and asked Maude where the dog's lead was. 'She has no need of a lead now,' said the maid, and so I left the house with the dog – loose! I hoped Maude was right. Had she really taught the dog to walk to heel in two months? We trudged across the estate and, only as we reached the gate did the heavens open, but Crumpet stayed by my side and we got wet together.

Given that I have lived in Ampney Tet for so much of my life, it was with a sense of shame – and very squelchy shoes, that I entered the village's library *for the first time*. (To be fair, the Ampney estate has such a generous library of its own, there has been little point.)

The building is located next to the school house and according to the words carved into its Cotswold stone, it used to be a pottery. I walked in, and was immediately struck by the amount of sunlight streaming in. Its large windows were a change from the Holloway prison library, which had had only the smallest, meanest windows at ceiling height, and the library at Ampney Tet – which always had the curtains drawn, to ensure the books didn't fade any more than they already have.

But this library housed all the latest romances, mysteries, thrillers, thesauruses, dictionaries and atlases; all thanks to the Dirigeon and Cullimore coffers. There was nobody at the counter, but there was a couple of women in the Religion and Philosophy section, discussing the whereabouts of a certain husband – or at least, one of them was. The other was listening, rapt, and they were both standing next to a notice that said, 'QUIET, PLEASE'.

'She said she'd heard that he'd been seen in Birmingham. "My Alan's brother's mechanic said so," she said, but I don't believe a word of it, because *my Alan's brother's mechanic* can't tell a Morris from a Rolls-Royce at a hundred paces, AND they used to drink together at the King's Head. Well, I said, it's much more likely that he's gone down to Devon, where his folks are from. And I say that, because I saw him heading to the station that last day he was spotted by anyone, and you wouldn't approach from Redding View if you intended to take the line north, would you?'

I rang the bell on the counter – to call for the librarian, and it was the talkative woman with all the news who looked over, said goodbye to her friend and approached the desk. She was wearing three pairs of spectacles. One on her head, one strung around her neck and one balancing on the tip of her nose.

'Good morning. I was just catching up with one of our readers, Eileen. She is a big fan of Hildegard of Bingen and she required my assistance locating her biography.'

'Mrs Burrows?'

'At your service, how may I help?'

'Actually, I was wondering about your job-finding service?' I said, and the woman's eyes widened, and she glanced around to check that there wasn't anyone nearby.

'Follow me, come this way,' she whispered, taking me into a little back room with a desk, a kettle, a couple of chipped cups, a pile of books that evidently needed some repair and a bookcase stuffed full of what? Notebooks?

'It's a service I like to keep separate from my library work – which is of course, my principal source of income, and very welcome too,' she said, nervously. And it was clear that Mrs Burrows wasn't supposed to be running an employment agency from the premises of the local library. 'Any idea of your words per minute?' she asked, looking me up and down. 'Do you have shorthand? Or are you a home carer? Plenty of call for them hereabouts, although you might be a little old for some of our customers... And I don't suppose you drive, because there's plenty of call for that – especially if you have your own motorcar?' She reached for an application form, and I stopped her in her tracks.

'I do, thank you, but actually, I'm here about someone you found recently – for Mr Cullimore.'

'Oh, Mr Cullimore, bless him. Yes, he was a man we found lots of helpers for,' she said, 'And gardeners, drivers, all sorts. The only member of staff he stuck with was his cook, and she's almost as old as he is – was. And what a shame that was, with him falling ill at that fancy do at the big house, but as I always say, there's none so–'

It was a miracle that Mrs Burrows had been taken on in an establishment were the ability to keep quiet was usually a prerequisite. 'Actually, it was his nurse, I was most interested in,' I said.

'Oh yes – well, she's already found a new job, so she isn't available,' she said with a look that suggested she was not impressed.

'I just wanted her name. I have some questions I want to ask her about Mr Cullimore.'

'Oh?' Mrs Burrows looked at me hungrily and, rather than have my enquiries be the subject of her next conversation, I told her that I was interested in the old man's stamp collection. It was the first thing that came to mind – and that was when I saw the water-damaged Volume III 'Stamps of the World' over her shoulder.

'Oh, well that's different,' she said. 'I'm a keen philatelist myself –'

'I'm sorry, I'm in a bit of a rush. A dentist's appointment, so I wonder if you could just –?' Lie after lie after lie. If she asked me which dentist I was going to, I was going to have to change it to doctor and toddle over to Dr Ferguson's for no good reason. Fortunately, she didn't.

'Well, you're in luck,' she said, consulting a calendar on the wall. 'It's her day off, her name's Loretta Shields, and she's back at the Red Lion.' I noticed four identical calendars on the wall, and that they were covered in initials and numbers – the people she employed and the times they worked. One was labelled

"Gardeners & Drivers", one was for nurses and companions, another for cooks and another for "Misc.".

I thanked Mrs Burrows for her assistance and, much as I would have liked to have applied for a library card, my ears were throbbing. I would try another day. I was relieved to see Crumpet waiting for me outside, and we headed down the street in search of Miss Shields.

(It was still raining.)

ELEVEN

The Red Lion is one of those pubs that should be on a picture postcard. Its flower baskets always have something colourful in them regardless of the time of year, they are happy to see you arrive, and sorry to see you go; and if their food and drink were half as nice as its staff, it would be a place worth spending time in. I entered the ladies' lounge with Crumpet and we both stood in front of the fire and began to steam, gently.

'Anything I can do for you, madam?' said a bright, young voice.

I turned to see a halo of red curls, peachy cheeks, a dimpled chin and a warm welcoming smile. Without her hair scraped back, and her nursing uniform on, Loretta Shields looked very different from the last time I'd seen her, but it was she, in all her voluptuous beauty. Her silhouette was far removed from the current fashion for straight up and down and, in truth, she looked like she harked back to an earlier age.

'What would you recommend?' I asked.

'We have hot soup!' she exclaimed, and she said it with such enthusiasm, that I didn't have the heart to ask her what it was. (Anything other than my thanks would have been an insult.)

And so, I accepted her offer of soup, asked for a sherry while I waited, and a little something for the dog.

She brought a lamb's ear for Crumpet, a glass of something warm and brown for me – and five minutes later, she reappeared with a hot bowl of something beige.

'Excuse me?' I said, 'Didn't you work for Mr Cullimore? Loretta?'

Her face fell, and her smile vanished.

'Yes. Or at least, I was until that party,' she said quietly, lowering herself into the chair opposite mine. 'What a lovely old man, Mr Cullimore was. He really enjoyed watching me dance and he was so encouraging about my singing. He was going to help me go on the stage. We were going to make it formal, like, but things change…' said Loretta, with a cheerful shrug. 'He told me he'd heard lots of nice girls sing and that he'd never come across a voice as nice as mine, and that's why he helped me out with my singing lessons.'

'Really?' I said, very glad that I didn't have Maude at my side. Her harrumph would have been heard for miles. 'I'm Georgie, by the way. The ball was at my uncle's place, and I understand you were Mr Cullimore's nurse?'

'Oh, I wasn't really a nurse – I mean, I was to Frank, but he said not to worry about my qualifications. We met when I began serving here, you see, but I was already on Mrs Burrows' books, so I told him he had to hire me through her – do it all properly. And he said that there were certain things he liked to have in writing, and certain things he wasn't bothered about.' She smiled a little too bravely, and then her smile turned upside down, and her eyes began to water. 'But maybe he wasn't quite right about that,' she said, and slow tears dropped down her cheeks.

I recalled that Mr Cullimore had been with Lettice when he'd died – and only when Mr Cullimore was clearly past the point of needing a nurse, had anyone been able to find the pretend one. Loretta, the nurse with the tangle of hair decorated with orange leaves. But who had she been with?

'You called him Frank,' I said.

'He was Francis to everyone else, but he liked to be "Frank" with me. That was his little joke.'

'I see.'

'And he said he could tell that I was a caring person as soon as he saw me – which was why my qualifications weren't a problem.' She took a deep sigh. 'He always made sure to eat an apple a day – and he was very serious about laughter being the best medicine.'

'Oh, yes?'

'Part of my job was to tickle him – for his health.'

I felt I'd probably heard enough, but I had to ask who she'd been with that evening although I didn't want to embarrass her. 'I gather you made a friend at the ball.'

'There were lots of nice people there – so smart and glamorous. And there was me in my uniform!'

'But I gather someone rather liked your uniform, didn't they?'

She got up from her seat, and began wiping my table. 'As I say, there were lots of nice gentlemen there. Such a grand house.'

'I'm sorry, it's just that I noticed that you weren't with Mr Cullimore, when he became ill.'

'I was there all the time!' she said, pouting. 'I... I may have left to get him a bowl of trifle or something. And I had to eat too. It's no good a nurse falling down faint with hunger and not being able to help when she's needed, is it?'

I agreed, but Loretta hadn't been there when she was needed by her employer, and I also recalled the spot of blood on her uniform when she did turn up.

There was no point in asking her any more questions. Loretta's colour was up, and she was angrily jabbing at the table next to mine with a soup-wet cloth – which isn't a very effective way of cleaning anything. I was about to leave when I remembered the bowl of soup. In my present fiscal predicament, was I really prepared to waste two shillings?

'Thank you for your time,' I said. 'And sorry for your loss. Um, this soup, is it Brown Windsor?'

'It's carrot, madam,' she said, before returning to the kitchen.

I decided I wasn't hungry after all.

I left the pub with Crumpet at my side – apparently the lamb's ear hadn't been worth nibbling either – and we trudged back in the drizzle, up the hill, to the estate. Under any other circumstances, it wouldn't have been the most enjoyable walk, but I had a spring in my step. I had learned some valuable things. Unless Mr Cullimore's will said different, the loss of Loretta Shield's employer was of no benefit to her at all. I had also learned that Mrs Burrows was a useful source of information; and a good way of spreading it too.

My heart did a somersault at the thought of the librarian being invited to one of my aunt's balls – and the stories she would have come away with. And it did another somersault when I considered what would happen if she ever got her hands on Bettina's manuscript.

Twelve

The manuscript was nowhere to be found in the house, and the only possible answer was that it had been taken by accident. Or stolen. Given that it was a red file with golden lettering, the former seemed unlikely – I had already contacted the Jazz Misfits – which left me with the latter. Who would steal Bettina's draft? Two types of people immediately came to mind – readers – overly enthusiastic fans who wanted to be the first to be privy to Bettina's "Purple Velvet" series, or the subjects of her work, who wanted details of their private lives kept out of print. Bettina had refused to divulge any names, so her fans were the subject of my enquiries.

I asked Maude for the guest list (yes, she did have it all written down), and I began to mark the innocent. Uncle Lawrence and Auntie Bathsheba – tick, Georgiana Mortimer – tick (odd that I was entered under my married name – until I recalled that my aunt had been keen that the ball NOT reflect my return to "surplus" womanhood. And besides, I rather liked the name and the "Mrs" too). Maude – tick (not actually invited, but most certainly there and partaking of the champagne). Bettina? Presumably she had not stolen her own manuscript, so – tick.

And Lettice and Jack? They had spent as much time as anyone, looking for the manuscript when they could have been doing a hundred other things. We were all sick and tired of turning cushions and peering into vases. And from what little I knew of their books, their writing style was very different and it would have been an awful lot of work to have ripped off one of her stories. They were also friends, and just as invested in the success of the Love Lost & Found Publishing Agency as Bettina and my aunt were. Jack and Lettice, tick, tick.

I went down the rows and rows of locals I knew, who I immediately struck off my list of possible plagiarists or fans. I couldn't know that they weren't regular readers of my aunt's literature, but, well, many of them just didn't seem *likely*. I watched as my aunt ticked off the ladies of the "fan club", who were also the ladies she regularly played bridge with, and I ticked off the Late Mr Cullimore. If he'd had the manuscript on him when he'd died, I'm sure Inspector Routledge would have mentioned something by now. Aunt Bathsheba also ticked off all the printers and publishers on the list who'd been invited by my uncle, despite my protestations that they were the very people who would have been most interested in such a piece of writing. But no, she was adamant that they were not to be included.

Roger Elton was ticked off the list: I was fairly sure that while Mr Cullimore had been fighting for his life, Roger had been tending a bloody nose. And the locals I didn't know? As I scanned the invitation list, I wondered whether it included the man I'd encountered in the stables? I had no idea of his name, although I was fairly sure, from what I'd felt of his jacket, that he hadn't been hiding any bulky paperwork. But a bottle of tablets, perhaps? I hadn't felt anything like that on his person either, and given the time and place of our little meeting, he remained a mystery.

The crowd in the billiard room had been all too familiar; it had to have been one of them. Old Cullimore hadn't left the room all night, and certainly nobody in attendance had worn a linen shirt. Whoever he was, he got a double tick for innocence on the part of the manuscript and the murder, although I pondered how I might find out who he was from Inspector Routledge. He was bound to know! One professional to another, if I asked very nicely might he tell me who –? My ruminations were interrupted by a sharp bark. Crumpet was standing in front of me with a look that seemed to suggest I was wasting my time. And also, a reminder that I'd veered into wondering about the murder and the man, rather than the manuscript. One thing at a time; I turned back to the list.

None of the locals, were of particular interest; pig farmers, brewers and small-town solicitors. The family from next door, the Ferveaux of Dirigeon, had been invited as per usual; a courtesy that was politely extended and just as politely declined. They were out of town.

And out of the non-locals, I ticked off all the Bright Young Things who'd been dancing to jazz and hadn't left the conservatory all evening. One of the more enterprising members of their party had sneaked into the hallway, where the food was, and had made off with a bowl of olives and a basket of fruit and that – along with vast amounts of champagne, was how they'd survived the evening. There was another group of people I had no idea about, and I asked Maude about them.

I caught up with her in the breakfast room, got us a cup of tea and we looked over the rest of the list together. She told me who the locals were that I did not know and which of them was likely to be unusually literate – or likely to benefit from the old man's murder. I asked her who on the list she did not know, and she admitted that, amongst the women, it was only Mr Cullimore's young nurse, who had been entered on the list as his "plus one".

'You know how madam likes to think herself artistic,' she said, 'Well, amongst the men on the list, your aunt invited a bunch of artists Betty knows.' (Maude was the only person in the household who dared to call Bettina that.) 'You know the types. Good for nothing layabouts who like to think themselves dangerous. Up to you if you tick them off or not.' She took a sip of her tea. 'Adlington I don't know, Bowers I'm not sure about – and Sutcliffe might be worth following up. They like to think they live for their art,' she said, as I topped up her cup. 'But would they die, or murder for it? That's the question.'

'Maude, I don't suppose you'd like to come up to London with me?' I asked. 'A little jaunt up to town might be interesting, you obviously know th–'

'A jaunt? A jaunt in the city? Go to London?' she said. (And I won't bother to describe the look she gave me, but I'll tell you this much, I almost fell off my chair.) 'Oh yes, and while I'm doing that, Crumpet here will run the fifteen-bedroom household, order about the staff and sort out your aunt – not to mention her townhouse and those cats of hers! I can't go faffing about in Mayfair. I've got far more important things to do.' So that told me.

I finished my tea alone and, as I folded up the list and tucked it in my handbag, it struck me that while I'd been ticking names off, I hadn't entirely made up my mind whether I was looking for a manuscript thief or a murderer amongst this lot. (And wouldn't it be handy if it were the same person!)

As far as I could tell, the likeliest suspects for the murder were still Cullimore's grandson, and great-grandson, whoever the young nurse had been with in the orangery and the mysterious Adlington, Bowers and Salter. I went in search of Bettina.

After twenty minutes traipsing about the upper echelons of the house, I asked my aunt where her Ladies were. 'Plotting in the stables, the last time I saw them.'

'Plotting?' I said, 'Are they working on a whodunnit?'

'More of a who's doing what, and to whom.'

'THANK YOU, Maude! How do you get about so stealthily? They are merely working out the relationships between all the characters in their books. There are so many of them, they need a little space to spread out all their notes, and a bit of fresh air is good for their grey cells.'

I found the three ladies petting Madrigal Girl –there was no sign of any work being done – and I asked Bettina who the guests were that she'd invited to the ball.

She told me that Leo Adlington was an artist and art dealer; quite a young man, good-looking. (I did my best to sound uninterested.) She told me that the last time she'd seen him the evening of the ball, he'd been heading out of the conservatory, onto the grass. Had he bumped into Loretta Shields and spent the evening with her, in the orangery? Or was there a chance that Leo had bumped into me in the stables – on the very spot I was presently standing? There was only one way to find out.

The "Bowers" on the list was Thomas Bowers, an art dealer, and a keen collector – and imbiber – of wine. She couldn't recall quite why she'd bothered to invite him, although she did mention that he was 'an old sweetie', but that she'd heard that his business was struggling.

And Salter? Bernie Salter. I asked Bettina what she knew about him, and she quickly corrected me. 'Bernadette? She's known as "Bernie" to her friends, and quite the catch. No money troubles because she doesn't care for the stuff, and I only invited her because I thought Jack might find her interesting – and I gather they spent most of the evening shimmying together, after she'd finished scoring at billiards.'

Jack said nothing on the matter, and strolled off in the direction of the lawns.

So, Salter was off the list – and definitely not the man that Loretta had spent the evening with.

When I caught up with my aunt at lunchtime, she said that Bowers and Adlington were both "in town" (just as Maude had said) and to ask Uncle Lawrence for the addresses because he knew everyone. So, I was off to London for the day. Baxter would drive me to Kemble Station, and I'd be in the Big Smoke – or the Big Peasouper (weather dependent) for elevenses.

I wouldn't normally have left that early, but my uncle advised me that the folks in Mayfair tended to have very long lunches. Whenever he had a meeting with any of them, he said that he always arranged it for some time before 12.15 (because they seldom returned to the office in the afternoon).

Thirteen

It was Maude's maid, Edie, who woke me up with tea, buttered toast and marmalade at half past six. Maude does mornings as much as my aunt does, and besides, I was in the cottage, which is a good two-minute walk from the side door.

''Ere you are, madam,' she said. 'Maude said not to give you the paper, or too much breakfast, because you'll need the time to make yourself look nice.'

I was *fairly* sure Maude hadn't intended for Edie to pass that on, but it was good to know, and Maude could be rather forthright when she wanted to be. Perhaps she had.

I struggled out of bed, and put a silk kimono on, and wrapped a mohair blanket around me. It was a cold morning. I sat for a moment at the window seat, and looked at the lawn sparkling with frost.

'Oh no, you don't have time for that resting malarkey. Maude said so. Drink your tea, eat your toast. And she suggests you wear the dark grey wool if you want to look serious, and the light pink if you don't. Your call.'

Crumpet more than made up for my lack of joy in the mornings (and Edie's lack of joy too), as she ran around the room, round and round as if she were trying to light it up, like some sort of doggy dynamo. When I said her name, she jumped into my arms. 'Oh no you don't,' I said. 'You're not coming to London with me – another time perhaps. You have to stay with Maude and Aunt Sheba. Your two favourite people!' The little dog buried her nose in her paws. Bathsheba and Maude together had implemented a strict training regime which, while impressive, must have been fairly gruelling for the little dog. I stroked her ears and put her down on the rug. Time to choose my outfit.

The navy crêpe de chine, with the dogtooth pattern? The cream wool? The purple damask? In the end, I opted for a flinty-grey wool with an asymmetrical hem that I found folded on the trunk at the end of my bed. It made me look just the right side of professional. When I'd said my goodbyes to Crumpet, Baxter took me to the local station and I read a super whodunnit written by Marjorie-something, for the two hours it took to cross the country.

When I alighted at Paddington at 10.54, I was starving. The cafe at Kemble Station had had some problem with its gas, so there was no tea to be had, and there was no buffet car being pulled by the train, so I left the station as quickly as I could, and found a Lyon's tea shop round the corner. I felt much happier, once I'd eaten my boiled eggs and soldiers, and I gazed out of the window at all the people passing by. Where were they going? Most of them were rushing somewhere, and heading wherever it was with firm intentions. The only thing I was doing with any "firm intentions" was eating a second breakfast. Given the recent turn of events, I wasn't sure I would get my job back at *Domestic Bliss*, the magazine I had worked for before my wedding, and Auntie Bathsheba had said something about an opportunity in her 'organisation' the day before I'd been released from Holloway, but she hadn't said a word about it since. It struck me that I'd learned a bit of self-defence and how to pick a lock while I'd been "away", but that sort of job would only land me back inside.

Questions about Mr Cullimore's unfortunate demise were the only thing keeping me busy at the moment (that and the missing manuscript). And so, with nothing better to do, I headed out, determined to enjoy the crisp spring day whilst keeping my mind on the mystery at hand – and off my present predicament.

Thomas Bower's gallery was in Mayfair, so I wandered across Hyde Park, down Park Lane, passed the Dorchester, made my way to Berkeley Square, sauntered across and arrived at Bruton Street with minutes to spare. I didn't actually have an appointment with either Mr Adlington or Mr Bowers, but I had decided I would make it there for 11.45; as per my uncle's recommendation.

Bruton Street is a marvellously swanky address made up of three and four-storey townhouses with smart porticos and freshly painted front doors, (although my aunt had been quick to point out that the properties I was in search of were not at the smart end, where the Earl and Countess of Strathmore were to be found). However, number 78 certainly wasn't the hovel my aunt had prepared me for; it was a smart little gallery specialising in Impressionism. A bell above the door jangled as I entered, and I was greeted by a rotund, red-cheeked man who puffed as he made it down the stairs at the back of the property and invited me to look around. I could have spent the next ten minutes feigning an interest in his small collection of French, late nineteenth century paintings by lesser-known artists, but I decided to get on with it. Time was ticking.

'Mr Bowers? How d'you do?'

'How d'you do?' he said, 'I'm afraid I haven't had the pleasure...'

'My name is Georgie-Georgiana Mort-Wre-Mortimer and I'm the niece of Lawrence Godfrey.'

His eyes lit up at the mention of the family name and he rubbed his hands together, and any pretence of hauteur was gone.

'I'm sorry, I'm not here to see your artwork – fine as it is. I'm actually here to ask about the ball at Ampney?'

'Oh,' he said, visibly deflating. 'Right, the ball. It was a shame that. I might have got some good contacts.' He took a deep breath and smiled ruefully. 'I'm not sure the English really appreciate the Impressionists – except for a bit of Turner, of course. They can just about manage him, and he started the whole thing off. But do they really even appreciate him? Do they really see what he was trying to achieve? And if they don't get William Turner, they won't get the French. Far too ephemeral. The folks around here like their art literal and on a plate. Literally on a plate. You see that gallery over there?' He pointed to the other side of the street and a discreet doorway with a large brass knocker. 'Timpsons. They sell still lives and they sell like hot cakes. Bit of dead fish on pewter? Can't get enough of the stuff.'

I gathered that Mr Bowers was a local of Ampney Tet, or rather, he had been until he moved to the Big Smoke – but he'd been waylaid by a deal with a possible buyer in Shrewsbury. It hadn't come off, and he had been so disappointed by the result that he'd returned to London, rather than stay with his sister in nearby Wickbury. So, Thomas Bowers hadn't attended the ball, and was one person who could firmly be said not to have murdered Mr Cullimore – or taken Bettina's manuscript. I left, clutching his business card, with a firm promise that I would pass it on to my uncle (who had more than enough pictures of gutted trout and dusty grapes).

Time to find 62e, and Mr Adlington. Where all the other doors were gleaming brass and fresh paint, this one was peeling badly. It did not of course mean that Mr Adlington's wasn't the most exclusive gallery on the road – far from it – but it was a surprise, nonetheless, and then I remembered that he was an artist, not a dealer. And the 'e' meant he was living in a garret right at the top of the house, in what would once have been the servants' quarters.

I rang the bell, waited, rang again, and finally rang a third time. There was no answer, and I was beginning to wonder whether Mr Adlington had decided on a very early lunch – when the door was opened by someone leaving the property, who told me that 62e was the topmost floor – and wished me "Good luck". I thanked them, and slipped inside.

I walked up the four and a half flights of stairs and when I got to the top, slightly flushed, I was surprised to see that the door to the flat was open. I took a moment to catch my breath and knocked, and peered inside. The apartment was as scruffy inside as the front door had been – but scruffy in a bohemian sense, rather than a needs-to-be-vacuumed sort of way. Paintings were stacked up against walls, there were statues covered in sheets, gilt frames, canvases and half-empty tubes of paint scattered all over the floor. 'Hullo?'

'You're early,' said a voice. 'Leave your clothes on the stool, make yourself comfortable and we'll get started.'

FOURTEEN

Following the voice, I entered the room at the end of the hall which was, I'm happy to say, very well heated. The man with his back to me, standing at the easel, wore baggy Oxfords, a rumpled, paint-spattered shirt and no beret, and his broad shoulders and wavy, brown hair vaguely reminded me of somebody. He turned – and his luxuriant beard was the first pointer that he wasn't the someone that I'd bumped into recently, in Ampney's moonlit stables.

'Oh, are you Wanda?' he asked, looking puzzled.

'No, no, I'm not,' I said, trying not to stare too hard at his powerful physique as he turned. His strength was all too apparent, and became obvious when I saw a stack of chisels in the corner. He was a sculptor as well as a painter.

'Ah, because I was expecting someone a little... rounder,' he said, wiping his brush. 'Never mind – you'll certainly sell. The stool's over there if you want t-'

'No, no, no, no, no, Mr Adlington. I'm not here to take anything off!' I said.

'You're not here for the job?'

'I –'. (I was certainly desperate for some sort of employment, but no, dear reader, this was not the sort of job I was prepared to take.) 'Actually, I'm just here to ask some questions about the other night.'

'Please, call me Leo,' he said with a flash of a smile. 'And you are?'

'Georgiana Mortimer,' I said, extending my hand.

He wiped his hand on a paint rag, and we shook. 'Hello Miss-Mrs Mortimer,' he said, glancing down at my ringed finger. 'We've met before?'

'No – at least, I don't think so. But you were at the Godfrey Ball- in Ampney.'

'The do in the Cotswolds!' he said. 'Great fun.'

I was about to ask him what he'd got up to when, out of the corner of my eye, I noticed sketches pinned to the wall. Most of them nudes.

'And I gather it was Bettina who invited you to the ball?' I asked.

'She's seen some of my canvases and sat for me too. I carved a bust of her recently, which sold surprisingly quickly. She's a very fetching woman,' he said, and he scanned the wall, unpinned a sketch and handed it to me. It was a charcoal study of Bettina; very well done, and I tried my best to look at it dispassionately. Her hair was loose, and she was glancing over her shoulder in a manner that was very tastefully done, and a lot less revealing than most of the drawings on the wall. 'Bettina said there could be possible patrons in the crowd, and she encouraged me to mingle. It isn't really my scene, but she thought it might drum up some interest,' he said. 'And a bit of cash is always useful.'

I could have told him that moving out of Mayfair would have made a big difference to his finances, but I could also see why he'd want to stay. The view over the tree tops of Berkeley Square, and across to the red-bricked Georgian terraces beyond was beautiful, and he was firmly in the middle of the London art scene – surrounded by galleries and auction houses.

But it also struck me that carving blocks of marble on the fifth floor was a bit of a dodgy undertaking, and my heart quaked a little as the floorboards squeaked as I took a step closer to his wall of sketches.

And as I examined the posed, relaxed, young, old, slender and Rubenesque amongst his models, I noticed yet another woman I recognised. It was a head study done in pastels, of a young girl with curly red hair, bright green eyes and peachy cheeks who, until recently, had been the nurse of Mr Cullimore.

'Bettina aside, we have another mutual acquaintance,' I said. 'A young woman by the name of "Shields." When he looked confused, I mentioned that her name was Loretta – and he still looked confused, so I pointed at the sketch.

'Ah yes, *Loretta*,' he said, as if I'd pronounced the name incorrectly. So, Adlington did know her name – and he was better at *looking* confused than I'd given him credit for. 'She's another very fetching young woman, and a singer of some promise, I gather.'

''Yes, she is. And until recently, she was the assistant of an elderly man.'

'The man who fell ill at the ball?'

'He did rather more than fall ill,' I said. 'It seems that Loretta's employer was poisoned.'

The man had turned his back as I spoke, and his reaction was difficult to gauge.

'That's quite something,' he said, jabbing colours onto the canvas. 'Terrible thing to happen at a dance.'

I'd come to tick the two Bruton Street men off my list, have a nice lunch with my uncle and spend an hour wandering around

Liberty's, but the artist's attitude wasn't as straight forward as I'd expected.

'The guest list had some people on it who couldn't be accounted for, which is the reason I'm here.'

'Here you are, indeed,' he said. 'And you're absolutely sure you don't want to sit for me, Mrs Mortimer? It's nice and warm.' And he smiled in a way that suggested he knew just how charming the effect could be. I lifted an eyebrow in reply, to which he asked. 'Well, if you're not going to pose for me, is there anything else you'd like to do?'

'Thank you,' I said, 'Another time, perhaps.' And I was relieved to hear footsteps coming up the stairs, and a female voice.

And as I left Adlington and Wanda to it, I headed off to the front door, but not before poking my head in the two rooms at the other end of the corridor. One was his bedroom, which was a lot neater and tidier than I'd been expecting, and the other was a kitchenette of sorts – although where one might have expected jars of jam and packets of crackers, Leo Adlington had bottles and bags of chemicals. The only thing I recognised was linseed oil, but everything else was unknown to me.

My uncle's absence from Ampney could only mean one thing (or possibly two, if you included his occasional forays into Westminster) – he was at the Paternoster's on Pall Mall, so I headed south.

Founded by regulars of Paternoster Row, the Paternoster Club is an ancient institution of leather-back chairs, cigar smoke-stained ceilings, hearty puddings and pies and ALL the latest newspapers, periodicals, bestsellers and worst-sellers (although the publications are generally admired for their bindings, typeface, paper and ink quality, rather than their use of language). A small regiment of discreet butlers ensure that the whisky flows freely, that the Great, the Good and the Very Well Off are well fed, and that their sweet teeth are seen to. And an equally discreet army of footmen and valets, ensure that their shoes are shined, their ties are straight, their trousers are pressed, and that there is a fresh room for the night – should they need one. And I imagine it is a room of monastic splendour. Starched sheets, scratchy blankets and tight apple-pie corners; just like Nanny used to tuck. And I imagine a great deal more besides, because, of course, despite my past in the publishing industry I have never set foot inside the club. I suppose I might be permitted to stand in the hallway and wait if I were very elderly or unwell, but women, really? It's my uncle's domain, and not a place I aspire to. Besides, we have our own haunts.

'So, Georgie, where are we off to?' My uncle had the air of someone who was bunking off school – he was a slightly different animal when my aunt wasn't around.

'Well, it is lunchtime...'

'Already?' he asked, peering at his watch. 'The Ritz it is then.'

I'm happy to say that Uncle Lawrence isn't a man who believes in half-measures and, if I can, I always arrange to meet him at around quarter to one.

FIFTEEN

We walked up the steps into the Ritz Hotel's grand, mirrored opulence and with a nod to the staff, we were shown to a table close to the string quartet – but not too close.

I treasure these moments with my uncle. When my mother's relationship with my father broke down, he stepped in; when I lacked family, he was there; when I needed help with schooling, he took care of it; and when my mother left on her travels, he provided me with a home from home. And much as I love my Auntie Bathsheba, whenever she's around Uncle Lawrence tends to melt into the background, so our lunches together are particularly special. He isn't a talkative man – and he is at his most voluble when he's riled up – but a carefully placed question over an oyster, often works wonders.

The waiter passed my uncle the menu, and I waved away mine; Lawrence always ordered for me, and he ordered well. Certainly, his tastes beyond the walls of Ampney Tet were far more sophisticated than anything Cook ever rustled up.

The consommé was divine, the salted cucumber was fresh and flavoursome, the poached salmon with parsley sauce was melt-in-the-mouth and the rhubarb tart was – very tasty indeed.

'I gather from your aunt, that you've been rather busy this morning?' said Lawrence.

'I have – oh, and before I forget, I've got this card to pass on. It's from one of the artistic types, who was supposed to have come to the ball. A Mr Thomas Bowers who's an art dealer on Bruton Street.'

'One of Bettina's invites?' he asked, with a raised eyebrow.

'He couldn't make it, and I was checking him out this morning.'

'Checking him out?' he said, with a raised eyebrow. 'Should I ask why exactly?'

'Auntie Bathsheba has asked me to find this manuscript of Bettina's.'

'Ah.'

'And while I'm at it, she'd like me to find out who poisoned Francis Cullimore.'

'Yes, she's afraid that my mother's garden will be dug up,' said my uncle, nodding. 'Well, the death of Cullimore is a rum old business.'

'And "old" he was,' I said.

'Exactly. Why bother to kill the man?'

'The usual reasons are money, love, power and revenge,' I said.

'Hm, and as regards the first, Old Cullimore was certainly "minted". I think that's the phrase, isn't it?'

I nodded. 'And I wonder who was in line to get it?'

'His only son died in a boating accident twenty years ago, which leaves his grandson Anthony, a granddaughter who married and moved to New Zealand, and the great-grandson…'

'Peter.'

'Yes, that's the one,' he said. 'Anyway, whoever inherits will be singing all the way to the bank.'

Something about what my uncle had just said lit a weak lightbulb in my mind... I nibbled meditatively on a *petit four*, and the mixture of pistachio and chocolate must have helped, because I thought of singing – and recalled the singer involved.

'The nurse!'

'Sorry?

'Mr Cullimore's nurse, Loretta, told me that Frank Cullimore was going to help put her on the stage – and that he was going to make it "formal".

'What? You mean he was going to *marry* her? But Cullimore was at least eighty years her senior!' (My aunt is a year and a half older than my uncle, and he's very sensitive about such matters.)

'I'm not sure that's what she meant,' I said, 'Although, of course, it wouldn't have done the nurse much good to get rid of him – Mr Cullimore was her bread and butter – AND paying for singing lessons. Which puts his grandson in a more precarious position, surely? He has far more to gain than anyone, assuming he was set to inherit.'

My uncle popped a *petit four* in his mouth and silently ruminated, but two can play at that game, so I popped another *petit four* in my mouth, all the better to ensure that he filled the silence. And he did.

'Perhaps.'

Ah. 'It's just that I was wondering if you might ask Stone if he could find anything out, probate-wise.'

'The man's on holiday at the moment,' he said, 'Although I shall endeavour to catch up with him on his return.'

I noticed that my uncle hadn't actually promised to find anything out, but it was a promise to do something at least, and with that I would have to be satisfied.

Lunch had been fairly light by my uncle's standards, but I bid him farewell on the corner of Piccadilly and St James's St, determined to try and walk some of it off. Our *rendezvous* had lasted longer than I'd intended but two months in prison had prevented me from seeing the latest in this season's hats, so I trundled along to Liberty's and did my best to look like a woman of means, rather than a window-shopper. By the time I'd composed a comprehensive list of all the hats I'd like to have if I suddenly came into money, I realised that I had very little time to get back to Paddington. Every cab that passed was taken, the Central Line was out of action and I was going to have to walk – or rather, run – to the station if I was to make my train. I also realised that I probably shouldn't have had all those sweet, little delicacies to finish off the meal.

I got to Paddington with minutes to spare before the five thirty to Kemble headed west. I lowered myself into my seat, cheeks red, huffing and puffing, and tried to calm myself, if only for the sake of the two ladies I was sharing the carriage with.

One of them managed a constant flow of chatter about a dog show they'd been to see, but I leaned my head against the glass, and tried to concentrate on the world outside. It had been a long and interesting day, but I was tired, and there was nothing I could do to block out the woman's voice. 'Oooh, and look, there's Wormwood Scrubs. Wasn't your Derek there?'

'He was nothing to do with Wormwood Scrubs!'

'I didn't say he was a *prisoner*, I meant that he was a guard!'

'I don't care if you did. He's never been anything to do with any of that nonsense!' she said, catching my eye.

I focused on the scene outside, and noticed we were passing a high brick wall. There was nothing to suggest it was a prison, but I realised she must be right. What would those two women have said if they'd known that, until very recently, I'd been in a prison too? And not as a guard.

When their chat finally resumed, I let their views on greyhounds, terriers and whippets, their local flower show, violets versus pansies and the best jam to eat in a sandwich wash over me again and, as the miles passed, I had time to think about what I had learned. That even working at a prison is regarded as a stain on some people's character. That Impressionism isn't as appreciated in this country as it should be, and that morbid plates of food still sell. Art dealers can struggle just as much as artists – who like to pretend money isn't everything, but do a very bad job showing it.

I had also realised that I will always regret the *petit fours* at the Ritz; not because they aren't incredibly fine, but because they are a nibble too far. That my uncle is a wonderful, if reticent lunch companion – and that there were people in Old Cullimore's life who could have benefited from his death a great deal, but whether they would have hurried it – slipped something in his drink – to make that happen, was up for debate.

Sixteen

According to Maude, Mr Cullimore's funeral was to be a very private affair held in the local church and, interested as I would have been in attending, I didn't feel I could. Besides, the last funeral I'd attended had been my own husband's – the event at which his first wife had been the one hiding in the bushes – and from which I'd been taken off to prison.

However, a quick trip to the library provided me with more than just a ticket and a little light reading. Mrs Burrows was on top form. When she'd finished finding a cookery book for one of her readers – and discussed the ins and outs of Mrs Andrews' surgery – she joined me at the desk, and I asked if she had any Agatha Christie. 'All out, I'm afraid,' she said. 'You know how people are; they love a bit of mystery, although of course, you won't do better than live in this village and be surrounded by it. Any idea how that nice Mr Cullimore died yet? Well, of course, I say "nice" Mr Cullimore, but the man could be fairly sharp when he put a mind to it. If you weren't in your twenties and built like a Gibson Girl, he could be quite terse when he wanted to be. Told me off, more than once – and me the librarian, in my own library!'

'But wasn't it his library?' I asked.

'His and the Dirigeon's,' she said, without missing a beat. 'But still, it's a shame he went as he did, although nobody's saying how…' (This pause was presumably to see if I could provide any information.) 'And his funeral today, up at St. George's and invitees only – as if such a thing were allowed – so hardly anyone will be there, least of all that girl of his – Loretta Shields – although I understand they're having a bit of a do at the Red Lion this afternoon, and I can only guess that that'll be his wake. For such a small, frail little man, he liked his ale and the regulars there will miss him bitterly, not least because he always paid for a round or two.'

So, the wake was to be held at the Red Lion. I returned to the estate and changed into the black skirt and jumper I'd worn when I'd been released from Holloway. Jack lent me a black beret and the two of us trooped into the village for an afternoon of fond reminiscences, a little, light snooping, and a glass or two of sherry.

As soon as we arrived, it was clear that the rest of Ampney had had the same idea. Given Cullimore's reputation for buying a round, there were high expectations that a free bar would go on all afternoon, evening and well into the night. We sidled into the Ladies' Bar and were surrounded on all sides by villagers holding plates of mushroom and chicken vol-au-vents, devils on horseback and other such exotic fancies, which definitely hadn't been made by the pub's staff. And fruitcake, which definitely had been.

'Don't you think we should have spoken to the Cullimores before diving into the buffet?' I asked.

'Nope,' said Jack. 'Have you seen this lot? If we don't eat something now, we'll regret it. Hand me one of those pastry things, will you?'

There was a queue of people lining up, to express their condolences to the Cullimore family – before heading in the direction of the food and drink, and it struck me that the locals could be very well-behaved when they wanted to. (That was before I noticed Mrs Johnson stuffing a plate's worth of food into her handbag.)

By the time Jack and I made it to Peter Cullimore and his father, Anthony, most of the food had gone, and I was glad we'd struck when we had.

'What a wonderful send-off,' said Jack to each of them in turn, before making her way back to what was left of the ham tidbits.

'So sorry for your loss,' I said to Peter, whose red-rimmed eyes were testimony to the occasion. 'And I would like very much to talk with you a little more about your great-grandfather, if I may. He was such a boon to this village.'

'Absolutely,' said Peter, with a sad smile, before blowing his nose again, 'It would be a pleasure to talk about him.'

Unable to think of anything better to say, I repeated those condolences to his father. Anthony Cullimore's eyes were also red-rimmed, although given the angle at which he was standing and the colour of his cheeks, I doubted it was grief that was affecting him. The table behind him, covered in empty pint pots, told a different story, and Anthony Cullimore hiccupped in reply. And so, seeing him at something of a disadvantage, I told him that his father had been taken far too young. '102 is no kind of age, is it? The man was in his prime!'

'Aye,' said a passerby. 'He trusted us to do the right thing by him, and here we are, at his favourite drinking hole. He would have loved this do. Shame he couldn't have been here to hear us honour him in the way we have. A TOAST TO OLD CULLIMORE!'

While I was wondering how much of their fondness for the man was related to his propensity for buying a pint, Cullimore the younger was mumbling.

'Honour,' he said. 'You want to know about HONOUR? And as for trust... the only people he did trust were these lot. Ha. My grandfather wouldn't have known honour if it had bitten him on the b-' But before I could tease some more details out of the man, a scuffle had broken out over the last plate of canapés; and I heard a familiar voice at the middle of it.

Five minutes later we were standing on the pavement, well away from the Red Lion, with strict instructions not to bless their house with our presence again. To her credit, Jack held a plate of cheese puffs in her hand. 'Want one?' she asked.

'No, I do not! Although I can't help feeling it's a shame they didn't have any steaks to hand,' I said, examining her burgeoning shiner. 'And I don't know how you're going to explain to Aunt Sheba how you managed to get a black eye at a wake.'

'Good job they were worth it then,' she said, popping a puff into her mouth. 'And where was that bar girl you mentioned. Old Cullimore's nurse? There wasn't anyone even remotely matching your description there. No titian-haired beauties in sight.' She was right, and I could think of no good reason why Loretta shouldn't have been there; besides which, I'd had questions I wanted to ask. She'd been at the ball with blood on her uniform, and when we'd met a few days earlier, I'd forgotten to ask her whose it was. Old Cullimore hadn't died of anything blood-related, but it was surely important. Where was she? And what had his grandson, Anthony, meant about the man's honour? I wasn't sure I'd have worked out the answers to those questions if we'd stayed, but Jack starting a fight over the buffet hadn't been at all helpful.

We moved under the eaves of St George's church, and ate the little pastries in silence, waiting for Baxter to take us home. So much for my investigation.

Seventeen

Following Peter's invitation to talk about his great-grandfather, I decided to pay him a visit, so, as soon as I'd had my bicycle ride and my lunch, Baxter drove me over. As we drove through the countryside, the sun began to shine (which made a welcome change) and a block of gold shone on the horizon. The late afternoon sun will do that to Cotswolds limestone; a soft, buttery stone at its best during the golden hour, giving a comforting glow to its surroundings.

And the building itself? Cullimore's home was only forty years old (according to Bathsheba), and this château – for it was built in the French style – was spotless. The ivy was pruned to within an inch of its life, the gravel was raked, the gutters were all in working order and the floral borders were straight and true. Cullimore's home was a picture of moneyed perfection. No wonder my aunt had reservations about it. Ampney Tet was lovely, but not perfectly so; it showed every year of its age, and was the reason my aunt and uncle worked so hard.

I had called Peter before I left, and I was duly greeted at the door by a butler, who took my coat and led me inside, AND IT WAS WARM. The house was warm in a way that I'd never known such a large space; a normal, even, spread-out warmth, unlike anything I'd ever experience in Ampney Tet. There – if there was any warmth to be had – it was being half-baked in front of a grand fireplace, turning oneself to ensure even-cooking. And I was basking in that beautiful heat, when I realised that the butler was waiting for me, at the bottom of a stone, spiral staircase. 'You'll find young Mr Cullimore at the top,' he said, before leaving me to it.

Of course, by the time I'd made it to the top of the turret, I was much warmer than was comfortable, and to describe me as "glowing" would have been a kindness. And when I'd caught my breath, I was reminded of my visit to Mayfair to see Leo Adlington's studio. Where Adlington's flat had been a wreck, with exposed lathe and plasterwork, and paint splatters on the floor, walls and ceilings, this could have been a gallery. Peter Cullimore's room was round (obviously) with a very grand four-poster bed in the middle, but otherwise, filled with watercolours – beautifully framed, resting on easels, amassed in piles or ripped into pieces and chucked into the coal bucket next to the small fire.

The man I had come to see was prolific, certainly, and was working intently as I walked in, but as I got closer, I was surprised to see that he was painting a portrait of Stan Laurel.

'Good afternoon, Peter,' I said. 'Sorry, I didn't mean to startle you.'

'Oh, Mrs Mortimer, I didn't expect you so soon.'

'Call me Georgie, please. And I see you're a fan of the pictures. Have you visited the Gaiety in Cirencester?'

'I enjoy going to the pictures,' he said, 'but I'm not sure what that has to do with my great-grandfather.' He took a step away so that I might get a better view of the portrait, and I nodded in an encouraging manner. Both Stan Laurel and Francis Cullimore were slight men, but there was an age difference of sixty or seventy years, and the nose, the eyes... He hadn't captured his great grandfather's likeness at all, and I wondered if all the portraits were quite as 'off' as this one – and then recalled the slightly dodgy and very numerous watercolours I'd encountered in the library.

Wandering around the room in appreciative silence, I tried to work out who some of the pictures were of. Was that Doctor Ferguson, or was it Mary of Teck? Mrs Burrows or Elsa Lanchester? It was hard to tell.

'I've been at it all morning,' he said, with a sigh, swilling his brush in a tankard of water – and leaving it there. 'I'll order us some tea.' Peter picked up the telephone and made a call to the kitchen, then, approaching a cupboard in the wall, he opened the door, pulled on the rope and sent the dumbwaiter down, and it returned to us five minutes later with a pot of tea and a plate of French pastries. No wonder my aunt had made a face when I'd told her I was coming here. At Ampney, if you weren't where the tea was it went cold, and that was that. And delicate French fancies? An Eccles cake, by all means...

He must have seen the look on my face, because he said, 'Only the best for my great-grandfather. The chef is Parisian, and it was he who prepared those nibbles for the wake yesterday. It's a miracle I'm not twice the size.'

'Although your father, evidently enjoys a tart or two.' I hadn't meant it to come out quite like that and realised there was some confusion on the son's part, but he must have realised what I meant.

'Oh, yes, yes, he enjoys his food, but not here, unfortunately. He and my great-grandfather had a bit of a falling out.'

'I'm sorry to hear that,' I said. 'Was it about anything -'

'The worst – and most ridiculous thing in the world,' he said, popping a whole pastry in his mouth. 'Money. I mean, it's just so silly!' he said, getting a brand-new brush out of a drawer.

(Easy to say when you live in a castle and have staff to bring you pastries, I thought.) 'So, where does your father live at the moment?' I asked.

'At the Ampney & Wold Gazette offices, on the High Street. He has a room above the printing press. Likes to get his hands dirty, and says that I don't!' He showed me his lily-white hands. They were, admittedly, covered in Payne's Grey, but I don't think that was quite what his father meant.

'And did your great-grandfather not approve of that line of work?' I asked.

'Oh, he doesn't-didn't mind any honest business, it was my father's headlines he didn't like.'

'Ah. And you're a painter I see. I've seen some of your work at the library,' I said, and thankfully, he took the comment as compliment.

'I've got a sitter coming later this afternoon, the vicar's wife, in fact. She showed an interest in my work and I'm always on the look-out for willing victims!' he laughed. And I laughed too. 'In fact, you might fit quite nicely into this outfit I've had made.' He opened the doors of a large wardrobe. And although it was bulging with clothes, it was immediately obvious that it was stuffed full of the finest tailoring. And from between the many suits, he fished a riding habit.

It was so exquisitely cut I wondered who'd made it, and I checked the label and noticed that it was a London tailor of some note.

'My great-grandpapa tried to buy a Singer-Sergeant at auction, but he was pipped at the post, so I said I'd have a go at reproducing the painting. I had this made for the occasion. It's so important with velvet to get the texture and light right – you wouldn't like to try it on?'

Peter Cullimore was absolutely right about the texture and light, but there was no question at all that the original had been painted in anything other than oils, and it definitely hadn't been done by a third-rate dauber. But there was something so innocent and excited about the way Peter approached the whole project, that I was happy to take part, not to mention the sheer loveliness of the garment.

'Who was this actually made for?' I asked.

'A... a friend of mine,' he said, 'It doesn't fit her any more.' It was obvious as he said it, that whoever she was, was the apple of his eye, and as he turned, I almost missed Peter whisper the words, 'An absolute goddess.'

Eighteen

I slipped into the studio's dressing room, in the eaves of its peaked roof, and I considered the outfit Peter had given me to try on. The velvet was of the highest quality, and not only were the sleeves, shoulders and lapels all hand-stitched, but the skirt's hem was too. And as the skirt of a Victorian-style side-saddle riding habit, it was made out of acres of fabric. I tried it on and had a twirl, and felt the skirt's delicious heaviness on my hips. It wasn't tailored to fit me, but a few pegs down the back held it as tight as it should have been, and when Peter saw me in the outfit, he clapped his hands together in the same way a young child might have done on Christmas morning. 'And now you must sit on a horse!'

There were probably a dozen things I should have been doing that afternoon, but wrapped in velvet, none of them came to mind, and so, I gingerly made it down the staircase, and told Baxter he could leave. Peter led me into the château courtyard, which was gravel, like the driveway beyond, and lined with beautifully tended bay trees in Chinese pots. The effect was stunning, and I felt far removed from the Cotswolds' rolling hills.

I heard the approaching clip-clop of my mount, and a bay mare was led out, and the rich brown of her coat shone even in the afternoon light. She was magnificent – and saddled up for a side-saddler, which is something I am not, although my aunt could have ridden her. While the stable lad held the horse – Flamingo-Daydream – still, I was provided with a set of steps to make it up to the saddle, and arrange my skirt as I tried to make myself comfortable.

'Your great-grandfather was keen on horses, then?' I asked.

'No, not particularly, said Peter, examining his charcoal sticks. 'I'm the one with the interest, but he was good enough to buy me a couple. He liked to say that the last time he'd taken any interest in riding was on the beach, at Weston-Super-Mare, and if there wasn't a bucket and spade involved, he wasn't interested.'

It seemed that the vicar's wife was all but forgotten, as Peter feverishly sketched and I gazed imperiously out of the courtyard's arches to the landscape beyond. Much like my aunt and uncle's place, the Cullimore home was situated in grounds designed to show it off to the greatest degree, and its lake and glades were very pretty. I could see why this had been the love of his great-grandfather's life – even if his house was a bit *"nouveau"* (my aunt's wording, not mine). But why not live in a new house? The lack of woodworm alone, not to mention the draughts in Ampney Tet – Oh the draughts!

'Um, Georgie? Georgiana! You're making a bit of a face. Are you all right?' Peter's words penetrated my ears and I realised I'd been daydreaming.

'Sorry about that. Is this regal enough?' I asked, gazing again, and Flamingo whinnied in a way that suggested I was fine.

An hour later, my 'seat' was numb, my back was aching, my gaze had dulled, and I could only imagine how bored the horse was. I was delighted to hear Peter say that the light was beginning to fade. He got up from his stool, and said, 'I've completed a preliminary sketch, and if you'd like to come and model again, I'd be most grateful.'

I had decided I wouldn't commit to anything until I'd seen his work, and I answered with a polite smile. As I was helped down from Flamingo-whatsername, groaning and tottering stiffly over to my host, it struck me that the Old Masters probably used props for riding portraits, rather than live, real-life thoroughbreds – and seeing Peter's sketch, I decided he could have done without the beautiful animal.

The horse he'd drawn looked like a loaf of bread on stilts and, even taking the voluminous, velvet skirt into account, the human figure (my figure) was at least twenty percent larger than it should have been, in comparison with the mare. My elbows were far too close to my wrists, and, even taking the angle at which I was sitting into account, my neck didn't sit centrally on my shoulders. And my face? I didn't have one. Oh! So, was I to sit as a body, and the face of the woman for whom this beautiful outfit had been created, would be inserted at a later date? I wondered who the "goddess" he'd mentioned could be.

I was relieved to see that my clothes had been brought down to ground level, and I didn't have to stagger up all those stairs to get changed, and with no Baxter to take me home, Peter offered me a lift, and I readily agreed. If his horse was this beautiful, how fine would his car be? I was surprised to hear the clip-clop of more approaching hooves (as my horsey companion was led away), and a horse and trap was brought around the corner.

'Somerset needs a bit of exercise, and I thought after all the sitting-still excitement of this afternoon, you'd appreciate a bit of speed!' he said, stroking the horse. 'We like a trot about, don't we, my darling?'

I was about to object, but Somerset had such a kind, sweet, whiskery face, I couldn't say no. There's just something about horses, isn't there?

Peter ran off to change into his jodhpurs, and I settled into the open carriage, with a blanket over my knees, when the vicar's wife arrived. Peter reappeared, and did a very good job of hiding his forgetfulness, and bidding me – and one of the footmen – goodbye, but not before Peter whispered into the horse's ear.

'I've just told Somerset where to go, and you should be fine.' The footman reluctantly took the reins, as his master returned inside, with his next model.

When we were far enough away that we wouldn't be heard by Peter, I asked the young footman if this actually worked.

'Telling 'm where to go?' he asked. 'I wouldn't know. Never been in charge of a 'orse' before. Never did anythin' like this when Ol' Cullimore was in charge.'

We certainly headed out of the estate in the right direction, but there was no speed about it and, when we got to the outskirts of the village, the horse took a left turn. I asked William if he thought it was right, and he looked confused and a little bit frightened, and muttered something about, 'This wouldn't have happened in Ol' Cullimore's day.' We were skirting the western edges of Ampney and, although we were strictly speaking, heading the right way, we weren't being taken in the most direct manner – but perhaps Somerset thought there was too much traffic in Ampney and had decided to take a different route? And then, just when I thought Somerset was going to take us all the way round the village, despite the footman's attempts at steering, Peter's horse took us back into town, up a side street, and we found ourselves outside a pub. And not just any pub; it was the Red Lion, where Loretta Shields worked.

It had, after a fashion, found its way "home", it just wasn't my home. The tavern was obviously a regular destination for Cullimores of all ages, and the son of the landlord came out with a bucket of water and an apple.

William the footman tied the horse up, and we headed off to the Post Office to see if we could use their phone to call for a lift back to our respective residences, and a stable lad.

And I thought perhaps I knew who the young woman was, for whom the riding habit had been sewn, and whose face would be painted by Peter – framed by a ring of red curls.

Nineteen

Settling down for lunch with my aunt and uncle, the following day, I was curious to know more about the Cullimore family. The old man's grandson, Anthony, was the current proprietor of the gazette, but had he been welcomed into the hallowed halls of my uncle's club?

'Allow young Cullimore into the Paternoster? I don't think so!'

I didn't think I'd ever heard my uncle speak with such passion, and my aunt was obviously just as surprised, because I saw a look of, well, of passion on her part too. 'Anthony Cullimore has been a thorn in the side of this community for years,' he said, spearing a slice of ham.

'Did he not go to the right school?' I asked. 'New money and all that...'

Lawrence snorted. 'Old Cullimore may not have had much in the way of schooling, but he became a man of great means. As for his grandson... well, I'm sure he knows his declensions. Went to that school on the coast. Winchester, was it? I don't recall. Anthony certainly had a great circle of influential friends when he left, according to his grandfather – and he could throw a ball, of course. Cricket or rugby; he was good for a game all year round. But none of it made him a leader of men, a man with any moral authority or a man of business.'

'Business?' said my aunt, making a face.

'Tish, tish, Bathsheba. Of course, the man is in business – as his late grandfather was before him – and business is necessary for the wheels of this country to go around. Need I remind you, that it's the families we know who haven't got something going on the side, who are having to demolish houses or sell them off brick by brick. Or even marry girls from Kansas!'

My aunt was about to say something, but her lips snapped shut and she made a muted little squeak. It isn't something Auntie Bathsheba likes to talk about, but her daughter-in-law, Louisa, isn't actually a "local", although she is coming along nicely. She doesn't come from Kansas, this was, of course, Lawrence's little joke, but her father's success is one of the reasons that Louisa is able to buy this season's must-have fashionable items, and that Ampney has any roof at all.

'Come now, Sheba,' he said. 'When a *business* – there, I said the word again – when a business has a fool at the helm, it will not go far. The efforts of the people below will be wasted; whether it's by the management's profligacy or a lack of forethought and loss of sales.'

I took a slice of game pie. 'So, old Cullimore –'

'- was at fault, yes. His wife, Dora was ill, and he thought that well-meaning staff and the right school would let him off the hook as far as mentoring Anthony was concerned, without considering how hard he himself had worked at the same age, and how much he'd learned before he was even allowed to set foot inside an office.'

'But someone told me that the Ampney & Wold Gazette is selling like hot cakes?' I said, and my uncle raised an eyebrow, and stalked out of the room, saying that he was going to look for some port. 'I feel like I might have missed something,' I told my aunt.

'It was the nature of the stories the gazette started to print when Anthony took over the reins,' said Maude, dishing out the beetroot. 'Made it more interesting to read – if you like that sort of thing – and twice as many people were buying it, but it was a bit tricky for some folks to stay in the village after certain stories circulated about public expenditure.'

So, Anthony Cullimore had begun printing articles that were popular, but which also explained why I had been one of the few people to shake his hand at the wake.

'I don't recall his father being particularly diplomatic at the ball,' I said.

'Oh, he wasn't,' said my aunt, 'But it's one thing to say that Councillor Adamson is an old goat, and it's another thing to print it – with evidence! And on that note, I think it's time for a small glass of sherry. Georgiana?'

'I'll go and get the decanter.'

Looking high and low, I pondered what she'd said. It seemed that the Cullimore family wasn't in everyone's good books, and it was time to do some research. (I finally retrieved the Amontillado from the stables. Jack had been enjoying a sip with a cheese sandwich, while fiddling with her motorcycle.)

I had returned to my aunt, with the decanter and glasses, when I heard the sound of gravel crunching. Coming up the drive, in all its long-nosed glory, was a rather dashing car – with Inspector Routledge at the wheel, and Lettice at his side.

I put down the decanter, only to find I'd poured rather more into my glass than I'd intended, and my shoes were soaked. Undeterred, I followed my uncle outside, with Crumpet yapping at my heels.

'The Sunbeam! Has the paperwork come through?'

'It has,' said the inspector.

'Glad to hear it, and about time,' said my uncle.

The car had been the source of months of anguish at the beginning of the year, when I'd driven it from the dreadful little cottage in which Edward had been murdered, back to Pimlico. And as a result of my wish to get away from the scene of the crime, the local magistrate had deemed me a flight risk, and I'd been imprisoned in HMP Holloway in the run up to my trial. Prior to my release therefrom, my uncle had, very kindly, purchased the car from my husband's first wife; a woman who did not drive, and who desperately needed the cash. And here it was, in all its long-nosed, oxblood-red glory.

Inspector Routledge passed my uncle the keys, and Lawrence was about to pass them to me, when he snatched them back. 'It's a little early in the day,' he said, 'And I get the distinct impression you've had one too many!'

'It was an accident!' I said, 'The decanter slipped!'

'I expect you'd like a sherry, Lettice. A little glass?' said my aunt, who was standing at the top of the steps.

'Yes, please,' she said, hurrying past me.

'Nice of the inspector to give you a lift from the village?' I said. 'Did you go anywhere special?'

'The police station,' she said. 'I was being questioned, but I'm free to go now.'

'Oh!' I wasn't sure quite what to say, but the shy smile, the deep blush of her cheeks and the speed at which she raced up the steps, told me that Lettice didn't want to talk about it at all.

I looked up at my aunt, who said something about it being 'a formality', and followed her employee in.

Anxious to go for a spin in my darling car, I offered to drop the inspector off at the police station, and as we sped along, Crumpet was good enough to stand guard on his lap, with her paws on the dashboard; all the better to assert her dominance.

'So, Lettice is a free woman now?'

'She didn't have anything of interest to tell us, and –'

'She doesn't seem like the murdering type?' I said.

'The doctor vouched for Miss Armstrong's state of mind at the time of the deceased's death, and I was inclined to take that at face value. I'm sorry to say that if we'd pressed her any harder, she would have admitted to the murders of Julius Caesar, Anne Boleyn and Othello. I know the type, and that's not the kind of confession we're after.'

Poor Lettice!

When we parked outside the station and the inspector opened the door, I realised that Crumpet wasn't on a lead. In theory, Maude had taught little Crummy to walk to heel, but of course, in practise she was doing nothing of the sort and it took three policemen and a passing newspaper boy to round her up in what had become a game. Crumpet has no road sense or respect for authority, and I ended up using my belt to restrain her; whatever Maude likes to say she's learnt. I suspect the only reason I got away without being fined for being a Public Nuisance, was because I'd given the inspector a lift back into the village – and he'd been given a bottle of priceless port for his assistance.

I tied the little dog up outside the post office, and crossed the road, to the office of the Ampney & Wold Gazette.

TWENTY

The printing press next to the Ampney & Wold Gazette's offices was busy, loud and dirty – and, even standing on its threshold, I was glad that I was wearing a grey dress, because I could feel ink in the air. I raised my hand to knock on the door to let them know that I'd arrived, but realised it would do no good. The printing press was just too thunderous, so I walked in, tapped on a man's elbow and mouthed the words "Anthony Cullimore", and he nodded and pointed in the direction of some stairs. I went up, walked through a door, along a small corridor, through another door, and as it shut, I could finally hear myself think. I was also standing outside Mr Cullimore's office.

And I was about to raise my hand to knock, when I realised that I wasn't sure what I was going to say, at all – and as I stood there, the door opened and the man in question, rushed out, bowling me over, but catching my hand just before I fell to the floor. Reminded of what my uncle had said about Anthony's sporting prowess, the older man wrenched me upright with a strength that was astonishing for his age – and let out a stream of colourful language that was also rather surprising. 'What the *jeffing doodah* do you *blinking* well think you're playing at standing right outside my *flippering* door?' (Not his exact words.)

'How d'you do? The Honourable Lawrence Godfrey's niece at your service' I said, gathering my thoughts. 'Although, actually, I'm here to ask a favour.' I rubbed my elbow to try to engender some sympathy, and I saw a flicker of concern cross his face. 'I've recently become a freelance writer and, although I realise my kind of writing isn't what you're after, I'd be very grateful if I could take a quick look at some of your recent editions, to see the kinds of things you do. I'd like to change tack, and -'

'And do what?' he asked, glancing at his watch.

'The archives,' I said. 'I'd like to see what the usual kind of Gazette writing looks like.' Was I even making any sense?

'The archives?' he said, pushing past me. 'Go to the Gazette's front desk – not the printing room – tell Mary that I sent you. AND YOU CAN BUY ONE OF THE *BALLY* THINGS WHILE YOU'RE AT IT!' And with that, he was gone, yelling something derogatory about the state of the front page to a couple of ink-smudged men, the tone of which made what he'd previously said to me sound caring. Anthony was a tricky man to like – and so unlike his quiet, sensitive son, it was hard to imagine how they'd managed when Peter was growing up. It was also hard to imagine that he hadn't got on with his grandfather. He certainly seemed to have the same drive.

Mary the receptionist, told me to take the stairs down into the basement, to a door marked 'Archives', and she left me to it. She also said that, as a guest of "Young Mr Cullimore", if I stayed until three o'clock, there would be a cup of tea and a biscuit coming my way. The room was dark and dingy, all the better to preserve the state of the newspapers, but it did make finding the ones you wanted a bit tricky. I returned to Mary's desk, and before I'd said a word, she handed me a small, pocket torch and asked for a penny to go towards the price of batteries – and a penny for the latest edition of the Gazette.

The first edition of the paper that I looked at in detail, was one of the most recent, and it included the obituary of Francis William Cullimore, born 1826. I learned from the article that his background had been every bit as impoverished as my uncle had implied, and that the man had risen to power and riches through hard grit, good timing and more hard grit. I could imagine that handing the newspaper (that he'd founded) over to his grandson would be a hard thing for Cullimore to do, especially as he had fought tooth and nail to make it what it was. And having his grandson, who had been given every advantage, then take his paper and turn it into something he had never envisioned – and lose him friends at the same time...

But Francis wasn't a suspect, and Anthony wasn't the victim.

Going through the archives, ten years back, the tone of the newspaper had been quite different; all the usual flower shows, local school concerts, Christmas pantomimes, choirs, cricket fixtures and results, Women's Institute meetings, agricultural fairs and a surprising number of séances. Council meetings and farmers' markets were also covered, giving their dates, times and locations, and details of Cotswold-folk born, married and buried were also a major feature. It was a very local newspaper that was useful, certainly, but only very mildly diverting.

When I hastily scanned a handful of papers printed in the last three or four years, all of those things were still covered, but they were certainly given less space. Instead, of "Local Hog Wins

LARGEST in Show 5 Years Running", the headline was more likely to be, "LIBRARY **NOT** FINE! Investigation Long Overdue: Councillor Cannot Explain 20% Loss in Library Funds". Another recent headline had been, "Merry Olde England? Or Merry Olde Building Site? Council pour Cold Water over Protesters' Hopes – and CONCRETE over Local Beauty Spots".

The grandson-run newspaper was critical of the many houses that the council proposed building on the outskirts of Cirencester, and I wondered how his grandfather had felt about that, especially since the obituary had mentioned that Old Cullimore had his thumb in a number of pies, including the local building trade.

It certainly explained why Anthony Cullimore wasn't well liked by certain locals, but it didn't tell me why his grandfather had been murdered; or why Anthony had said what he'd said at the wake, about his grandfather knowing nothing of truth and honour. Glancing at the clock to see when tea would be, I settled down to find out more.

Twenty-One

Absorbed in the piles of papers I was surrounded by, when Mary knocked on the door at three, I let out a yelp of surprise.

'Are you all right?' she asked, setting down a cup of tea and a single digestive on a very large plate.

'You took me by surprise,' I said. 'It's very quiet down here.'

'Hasn't been lately,' she said. 'It's been like Piccadilly Circus. Everyone wants to know the comings and goings of Ampney at the moment.'

She asked me if I had everything I needed and I was about to say, 'Yes, thank you,' when it struck me how slowly I was making my way through the archives. At this rate, it was going to take me weeks to find out anything. Adopting my best, most professional face, I asked if I could see the births, deaths and marriages files. Much quicker than scanning every single copy of the A & W Gazette.

'That's no problem. Now, if you wouldn't mind pointing the torch... thank you. Which year was it you were after?' she asked, turning the key in the cabinet.

'1865, 1926, 1875, 1911 and... let me see which others,' I said, reciting random dates – enough of them to be troublesome. I waited for Mary to say, *"I can see you've got quite a lot you want to inspect, would it be an idea for me to leave the cabinet open? And here's a jug of hot water for you to top up your tea, and an extra couple of biscuits."* But she didn't. 'Oh no. You can only have one year's file,' she said. 'It's the rules.'

'But-'

'Was it 1865 you wanted?' she asked.

I nodded and waited for her to unlock the drawer and fish the file out. 'And if you could leave it with me on your way out,' she said, putting the single file on the table, before locking the drawer, checking she'd locked it, giving me a bit of a look and reversing out of the room with her tea tray.

1865 was all very well – the year Old Cullimore had taken on the gazette, but it wasn't going to tell me half of what I wanted to know. Fortunately, a cabinet of this vintage was easy enough to open without any specialist tools, and a couple of bent hairpins would do the job nicely.

Marjorie, my lockpicking mentor at Holloway, had made me solemnly promise that I would keep practising, telling me that that the more I did, the better I'd be, so it was with a sense of duty that I applied myself to the lock. Having learnt this skill under moonlight, I wasn't put off by the gloom and found working with my eyes shut, further focused my concentration. Where the cabinet in the prison governor's office would have taken me 23 seconds (by the time I left prison I was pretty good), I'd been fiddling with this one for a minute and a half before the final pin clicked. I was out of practise. As I slid the drawer open, there was the beginnings of a diabolical squeak, and I recalled another piece of advice Marj had given me. With one hand keeping the drawer steady, and an outstretched leg,

I managed to loop my handbag strap over my foot and move it close enough that I could reach inside with the other hand, and get at the little tin of Vaseline in the pocket. Popping its lid with one hand took longer than opening the lock had done, and when it was open, I smeared a blob of it on my lips, and another blob of it on the runners. The tell-tale squeak was silenced.

And why did I want the births, deaths and marriages files for all those years? Useful and interesting as those dates are, I could have got them at the local church. But a newspaper's obituary files are a cut above, and they were labelled as being in the bottom drawer of the cabinet. That was where the real information was buried, and it was those files I really wanted to see.

It is perfectly normal for a local bigwig to have a file written about them, that covers their life as they live. Only as a person ages, are those files compiled into obituaries; the required 500 words – or longer (depending on their level of importance) that is printed when they shuffle off this mortal coil. In the meantime, those obituary files are the unofficial source on everything connected with the great, the good and the gruesome of a town, including the most banal and most salacious snippets of gossip. A valuable resource for anyone with questions that need answers. For anyone closely related to the person who's died, the final, authorised, printed obituary in a paper is usually notable for what it leaves out, rather than what's kept in; hence the need to see those unpolished files.

And what did I find out?

Francis William Cullimore married his wife, Dora, when he was twenty-six, and she was just seventeen. By this time, he was the part-owner of an abattoir, was writing articles for the gazette about the outcomes of local agricultural events, and he seemed to be well thought of in local circles, despite being taken to court once and made to pay costs in relation to a border dispute. Dora Cullimore, née Parker, was a local beauty of modest means, and their only child, a son christened "William", was born nine and a half months after their wedding; a honeymoon baby.

William married a Welsh woman, called Eleanor, when he was young – they were both young, and they also had one child, Anthony, born the same year, in 1873. When both William and Eleanor were killed in a freak boating accident a year later, their baby miraculously survived, and was raised by his paternal grandparents. The family suffered another loss, when Francis' wife, Dora, died after a long illness; when Anthony was fifteen years old.

In 1901, Anthony married a woman called Susan, and their only son, Peter, was born later that year. And Peter? He remains unmarried – at least as far as the local newspaper's file is concerned.

Searching further into the files and archives, I learned that Anthony's wife Susan married again three years ago and seeing as divorces aren't printed in the newspaper, I could only assume that she and Anthony had divorced, and were on amicable enough terms that he would allow his paper to print her change in circumstances.

Taking a moment to enjoy my tea, I took a little break from the Cullimore's and I looked up my uncle and aunt. It turned out that they'd been married a lot closer to the birth of their first child than I'd realised, and that my uncle had been engaged to a Swiss woman before he'd met my aunt, and that, before they had finally tied the knot, my aunt had been engaged too. FIVE TIMES in fact! I put the file away, before I found out anything I was likely to regret, and returned to my task.

So, putting the Godfreys to the back of my mind, what had I actually learned about the Cullimore clan? That the men in the family were oddly fecund, and that honeymoon babies were the norm, but just the one, no more. A family of lone boys – and Anthony more alone than any of them.

Anything else? From what I could guess, Old Cullimore hadn't approved of his grandson, Anthony's marriage. There was no wedding notice in the paper, although it had been inked into the obit file.

Had he thought them too young, perhaps? Although, I did my sums, and worked out that Anthony was two years older than his grandfather had been, when he married. And what of Peter's mother, Susan? She was a local beauty, of course, but ten years older than her husband, and not from a family of any note Could that have been the problem?

Had Francis Cullimore risen so high from his meagre origins that he wanted no part of that world now? It seemed unlikely; he wasn't shy of his background, from what my uncle had said. Did the old man feel that his grandson hadn't achieved enough to secure a wife? Was he shocked by his son marrying a woman so much older than he? The age gap was unconventional, but maybe more understandable in a man who had lost his mother at such a young age. (And really, what was wrong with it anyway?)

Looking further through the pile of paper in front of me, I noticed that Anthony had printed a whole page "In Memoriam" for his grandmother Dora, just one month after he'd taken over the paper, so he obviously felt her loss keenly.

But what did any of this have to do with Francis' honour? And was the motive to the old man's demise to be found in this pile of paper? Francis Cullimore's murder had been cool, calm and calculated, certainly, but how long had it been planned?

I'd spent hours in this dingy little room, and felt I was going to leave with more questions than answers. I took another sip of my tea, and realised it was cold. I was just smoothing a blob of Vaseline on my lips, when I heard footsteps approaching.

'How long has she been in there?' asked a voice – a man's voice. It was Anthony Cullimore, and he didn't sound happy.

Twenty-Two

'Mrs Mortimer has been in there since just after lunch,' said Mary, 'And I took in her tea at three.' I could hear her scuttling along in her employer's wake.

'She's been rooting around for four hours,' said Anthony. '"*A quick look at the archives*" my foot. What the hell is she doing in there?'

The table in front of me was piled high with newspapers from all sorts of years and, more importantly, the obituary files for Cullimore's entire family.

Holding the torch between my teeth, I gathered them up, shuffled them into a pile and shoved them into the bottom drawer, before slamming it and realising too late the noise it would make – added to which, it was a cabinet that had been locked by Mary, who was standing right outside. I jammed my fingers between the drawer front and the body of the cabinet, to muffle the sound – and was forced to bite down on the torch between my teeth, to muffle my pain. I gently closed the drawer as quietly as I could, turning my hairpin in the lock and taking a deep breath.

Cullimore's outline filled the door's glass, and his receptionist was also clearly illuminated against the corridor light, bobbing about in his wake. While the two of them took it in turns to fiddle with the door knob and angry words were spoken, I did my best to calm my breathing and ignore my throbbing fingers. I plonked myself down at the table, took the torch out of my mouth and jumped a mile high when the door slammed open, and the big man strode in. 'What do you think you're playing at?' Cullimore demanded. 'What is it you're after?' he asked, pointing a torch at my face; and then at every other corner and crevice of the room, checking what I'd been up to.

'I'm not after anything,' I said, as breezily as I could. 'Just researching local history, and determining the style in which the Gazette likes to inform its readers,' I said. When my eyes were able to readjust to the gloom, I looked down at the table, and realised I had managed to clear every single file away. 'In fact, I'm all done,' I said, attempting a smile. 'And thank you for opening the door, I was wondering about that. The wind must have caught it.'

I walked along the corridor and up the stairs, followed by Mary who peered at my bag as I left – presumably satisfied that it was too small to contain any of their publications. I passed her the torch and I had just made my way through the front door, when I heard the words, 'Wait! Mrs Mortimer? You borrowed 1865. Where is it?'

Ah! The 1865 was, of course, safely tucked, or rather, haphazardly stashed in the bottom drawer, along with all the other files, in a cabinet I had opened and shut myself.

My fingers still throbbing, I looked behind me to check that the newspaper's proprietor hadn't followed me out and, heaving a great sigh of relief, that was when I spotted a familiar little four-legged creature sitting on the pavement.

Someone had given Crumpet a scrap of blanket to sit on, a bone and a saucer of water, and she let out a single high-pitched bark. The little dog gave me a look I shall take with me to the grave. I poked my head in the post office, and called out "thank you" and, as I untied her, I heard snippets of conversation from within. 'Shouldn't own one if you don't look after them', 'Poor little mite', etc. I walked to the car with my dog in my arms, and my tail between my legs.

My fear of being found with the files had cleared, and been replaced with shame at my behaviour towards Crumpet who, by the time we made it to the car – and I'd allowed her to sniff a few corners, seemed fine and dandy, and a lot better than I did. She leapt up onto the dashboard, waiting for me to drive away, while I leaned my head on the steering wheel and took another deep breath. Was I responsible enough to own a dog? Should I have wiped my fingerprints off the cabinet? Would my thumb ever recover? What was I doing with my life? And was Anthony Cullimore hiding something? He was angry, certainly, but he had also been anxious to know what I'd been looking for. Had he hidden something in those drawers that I hadn't found? I couldn't face going back, and doubted that I'd be let in anyway.

I returned to Ampney, and bumped into Dr Ferguson in the hallway. He was just leaving after tending to my uncle's gout, and I was about to ask him about the investigation, when the telephone bell rang, and Maude answered it, and passed him the receiver.

After he'd taken the call, the doctor said, 'It seems that Mrs Todworthy has had a funny turn, so I'll have to dash,' and off he went.

'Has he gone?' asked my aunt, her voice ringing from the library, 'I wanted to ask him about Cook's elbow...'

And I was reminded of my own thumb – the tip was reddy-purple, and I asked Maude for some iced water.

'Too close to dinner, now, surely?' said my aunt, but she seemed satisfied when I popped my thumb in the cup, rather than drinking it – and then didn't seem to notice when I was brought a cup of tea, shortly afterwards. I was parched and grateful for the drink after a decidedly dry afternoon spent rifling through musty old papers; and then the nasty and exhausting turn it had taken.

'How is Uncle Lawrence's toe?' I asked.

'Absolutely fine, in fact, a lot better than your finger from what I hear,' she said, brushing aside my concerns, 'But what is much more interesting is the recent news on the Cullimore front! Ferguson says that the coroner has gone over the paperwork and the verdict might be changed, from murder to "death by misadventure".'

'Really? I must say, it's a little surprising they didn't come over to see me about it,' I said. 'I was a little worried that with my background they might hone in on me.'

'Well, it's a measure of how badly trained they are in this locale, that they wouldn't *immediately* want to question you, given your background,' said my aunt, with a raised eyebrow. It was pointed and a little on the malicious side, but not to be argued with. Had my uncle had a word with them?

'According to Mrs Burrows, the Police Laboratory hasn't been as thorough as they might have been,' said Maude. 'The samples have been lost and that might be an end to it.'

'It would be one less thing to worry about,' said my aunt. 'And it would leave the constables no reason to poke about in my walled garden.'

'Have they been back?' I asked.

'No,' she admitted, 'But they could have been.'

'A mistake in the paperwork is hardly confirmation of innocence,' I said, 'But as long as Inspector Routledge is convinced…'

'And you're not?' asked my aunt. 'You know, if the police are satisfied, you really don't have to go on with this.' She looked at me in that strangely, calculating way she sometimes has. We both knew that this little mystery was putting off the day of reckoning; when I would have to return to London and really think about my next move; a job, a home, a future. (I would have to make enough money to keep Crumpet in blankets and bones, at the very least.) There followed a pocket of unfilled silence.

I had given my aunt the chance to say something about the opportunity she'd mentioned when I'd been about to leave prison – and she hadn't taken it. So, clearing my throat, I said, 'You know, there's more to Cullimore's death than meets the eye.'

'That's the spirit,' said my aunt.

'And still no mention of the will,' I said, realising that there had been no mention of beneficiaries in the obituary that the Ampney & Wold Gazette had run on Mr Cullimore. It wasn't standard practice in the city, but country folk could be fairly calculating.

'Mm, I was wondering when you'd get round to that. It seems there's been a mix up with that paperwork too.'

'*Another* mix up?'

'Local solicitors,' said my aunt, with a shake of her head. 'Cricklethwaite, Dingle & Stone would have been on it like a pack of hounds, but Mr Tolliver isn't the man he was.'

'And even then, he wasn't the man he should have been,' said Maude, taking my cup.

'Indeed,' said my aunt. 'It seems that there are two of them, an old will and a more recent one, and at one point he had neither of them, and now he's just got the one.'

'Which one?' I asked.

'I've no idea,' said Auntie Bathsheba. 'Oh, and talking of things that are missing, have you talked to everyone in the fan club about Bettina's manuscript?'

Twenty-Three

Concerned about the old man's murder, the whereabouts of Loretta Shields (who hadn't been seen since I'd talked to her at the Red Lion) – and the fate of my aunt's poisonous walled garden, of course, I had completely forgotten about Bettina's manuscript.

'I hope you're still looking for that literary gem, because it won't find itself, you know,' said my aunt. 'And the world will be a poorer place for its absence.'

'Bettina didn't mention her manuscript when I bumped into her two days ago, yesterday or this morning,' I said.

I heard a snort, and noticed Maude arranging some flowers in the hallway.

'I'll thank you to keep your thoughts to yourself, Maude,' said my aunt, and she urged me to visit the half a dozen Ampney society women who made up her fan club. I skipped lunch, when the maid assured me that the rest of my day would be a round of tea, cakes, nibbles and probably a glass or two of something, and rather than drive myself, I asked Baxter if he would accompany me.

Mrs Euphemia Nash was my first port of call. She was known

as "Effie" to her friends, and I wasn't sure that I'd got the right place, when I turned up at the address my aunt had written down. Foxglove Cottage was barely visible, located as it was in the middle of a small English jungle. I battled through the foliage, and made it to the door, where there was a small hand-written note attached to the dull brass knocker, which said, "Please use the bell energetically". I rang an ivy-twisted rope and heard a distant bell but got no response, so I tried again with some vigour, several more times. The door was eventually opened by Mrs Nash herself – she appeared to have no maid – and I was invited in. I recalled the woman from the ball, from the billiard room, in fact, because her great pile of haphazard, white hair was hard to forget.

Entering the property, I was surprised it wasn't bigger, given the size of its plot, although this impression may have been something to do with the way Mrs Nash lived. The entire place was FULL of the weird, the wonderful and the wildly extravagant – none of which had been dusted in a very long time. Brightly-feathered, stuffed birds peered imperiously through cobwebs, from the tops of Chinese bookcases that zigzagged up the walls, while wooden masks judged visitors as they entered the hallway, and wiry-limbed sculptures walked up the stairs. There was barely any space to be had, and when it was clear that I would require a seat, my hostess took a glass case containing a penguin from one armchair and settled it onto a pile of paperbacks on another, next to an armadillo that had seen better days. The place was piled high and teetering. While I was enveloped in dusty chintz, a broken spring poking my backside, Mrs Nash settled into a throne – there's no other word for it – an enormous carved, wooden chair with flaking gold leaf. It looked distinctly mayoral.

'You've come about the cooking job?' she said, in a voice that rang out, and that I vaguely recalled hearing at the ball. 'It's been sardines on toast ever since Annette left, so I'm ready for a change. Now, it's been a little while since I've had staff, but I think you'll find me a fair employer. Firm but fair.'

'No, Mrs Nash, I'm Georgiana Mortimer – the niece of your friend, Bathsheba,' I said.

'Cooking and cleaning?'

I shook my head, and looked around for a pencil and paper, but could see nothing useful. She must have seen the confusion on my face, because she reached behind the cushion on the throne and drew out a small ear trumpet – and conversation could begin.

'So, you're Bathsheba's girl?'

After a sneezing fit, I was able to introduce myself and tell her that I was indeed Bathsheba's niece.

'Don't suppose you'd be up for a little bit of cooking and cl- No? I quite understand, but I thought I ought to ask. The advertisement's been in the gazette every Thursday for the last two years, but I've got nowhere with it, and I've quite given up on Mrs Burrows. Never mind. Would you like a cup of tea, Georgiana? A nibble of something? I'm sure I have some biscuits somewhere.'

I moved my hand, and saw a twirl of dust rise into the air, illuminated by the afternoon sunlight. 'I've just had one, but thank you.' I explained that a manuscript had gone missing, and that my aunt had asked me to help with enquiries.

'The famous, stolen manuscript!' she said.

I hoped fervently, that it would not turn out that Mrs Nash had it because how it would be located in this enormous pile of STUFF that she called a home, I couldn't imagine. As long as one sat very still, it was interesting to look around, but as soon as one moved, the dirt was unruly, and I wondered whether there was a Mr Nash hidden in a corner somewhere.

'Is there any reason why you think the manuscript was stolen?' I asked, 'And can you think of anyone who might have wanted to take it?'

Euphemia's eyes flashed. 'Well, from what I hear, my dear, it could have been any number of people, and that's rather the point isn't it? A work of such thrilling importance – a classic! After all, Bettina's capable of anything.'

'Anything?' I asked.

'Well, I'm not suggesting she did Old Cullimore in, or anything like that, I'm just saying that she's very capable.'

'*I* wasn't suggesting she'd poisoned anyone!' I said, feeling slightly aggrieved.

'So, it WAS murder!' said Mrs Nash, rubbing her hands together. 'I knew it!'

The question was not how Mrs Nash had known it, but how she *hadn't*. The village had been full of the news as soon as Dr Ferguson had found out. He wasn't a discreet man.

'And I don't suppose you know who might have done it?' I asked.

'Oh, any number of people could have done him in,' she said, airily. 'He wasn't well liked, although he certainly had an eye for the ladies – for as long as it suited him, at least.'

'Any in particular?' I asked.

'I'm just saying that I wouldn't have been holding hands with the man, if I'd been Lettice.'

Twenty-Four

I left Mrs Nash's house, and slapped and flicked my dress as I walked up the path, desperate to get rid of the dust. I was headed towards the Sunbeam, but Baxter took one look at me and I stopped where I was, heartened that he already cared for my tourer enough to want to protect it. A minute later, he'd laid a blanket on the front seat, and handed me a clean cloth and a flask of water. I wiped my face, and hands, and flicked the cobwebs from my hat, hair and shoulders.

'Am I clean enough to visit the next one?' I asked. 'Who is it?'

Baxter consulted the list I'd given him, and told me it was the Honourable Honoria Somerton – and that I would do very nicely. As I got in the car, I asked Baxter what he thought of Old Cullimore; I might as well get as many opinions as possible. He sat silent for a moment, and then said he would give it some thought – which is never a good sign, is it?

It seemed that Old Cullimore hadn't been as well liked as I'd imagined, and then I wondered who I'd got that favourable impression from. Auntie Bathsheba didn't seem to have known very much about him. Uncle Lawrence was impressed by how well he had managed his business, but hadn't actually said that he'd liked the man. Loretta Shields – well, she was employed by him, and he was 102 when he died, so there was a chance that he'd mellowed in the last couple of years, at least. Then again, in 102 years one might make more than the average number of friends and enemies.

I arrived at Somerton's townhouse in the middle of Ampney and, when I tapped on the door with the brass knocker, I couldn't help seeing that it was some kind of Pan-like creature's head. Rather sinister, and a world away from a WELCOME mat.

The door was opened by a maid, and I was relieved to see a clean and entirely ordinary looking home, with just the right about of decoration, furniture and entirely local taxidermy (a squirrel, a fox, a rook and a fanged hedgehog).

'If you'll wait here,' said the maid, 'I'll just let Mrs Somerton know you've arrived.'

The corridor was lined with a long Persian rug, and on one side, there was an Indian tapestry, and on the other, a narrow hall table, decorated at its corners with golden sphinxes; but it wasn't that, or the needlework that caught my eye. There was a Japanese etching which was much more arresting and I swayed my hips this way and that, trying to work out exactly what the couple was up to.

'Ha! I regularly spend stolen moments trying to do that myself,' said a voice from above, 'I won't be two ticks. Just putting some lippy on!' Two storeys up, there was a silver-haired head looking over the balustrade. The maid returned, and said that madam would be down presently, before unceremoniously plonking my hat and jacket on the Chippendale, possibly in response to the extended time I'd taken looking at the etching, trying to work out the angles.

I was ushered into the breakfast room, which displayed no nudes on the walls, in fact no artwork at all, but had a very lovely view across the graveyard to the golden stones of St Peter's. I was soon joined by Mrs Somerton, who I also remembered from the ball; one of the small group chortling loudly with Lettice, and a woman whose taste in lip rouge was exquisite. (Crimson and so glossy.)

'Please, call me Honoria,' she said. 'So nice to entertain someone who doesn't tut when they see my art – not that your aunt or her writing ladies, are likely to do anything as dull as that. Tea?'

Having missed out on anything to drink at Mrs Nash's house, I said 'Yes, please,' and got down to business.

'It is all rather racy isn't it,' she said, 'A stolen manuscript!'

'Why do you say "stolen"?' I asked, taking a sip of my tea and coughing violently. (I hadn't realised how dusty my throat was.)

'Well, it MUST have been taken – a thing like that? I was shown the red file at the beginning of the ball, I was one of the first to arrive, and I have been a long-time fan of your aunt's publications. I was there right at the beginning, I bought their first pamphlet, and as such, I was one of the first to be told about the little gem, but by the end of the night there were rumours it was gone. Somebody at that party made off with it. And what with the murder of old Cullimore, it was quite a night all round, wasn't it?'

'May I ask, who told you that the manuscript was gone?'

'Well, let me think… it was definitely after the murder. A young man with a bloody nose ran into me just after we heard the scream and he sent me flying, and I must have spent the best part of five minutes with one of your aunt's maids trying to get his blood off my beads. Fortunately, the dress is the colour of ruby port, but I don't like to think of having anyone's O, A or B on my person – especially given the hunt the next day.'

I thought perhaps, that young man with the bloody nose might have been my doing, but I didn't say so. There was no need to introduce Roger into my enquiries.

'And as for who told me about Bettina's writing going missing, it might have been Lizzy Hampshire. Or it could have been Freddy, of course. More tea?'

Over a second cup, I asked Mrs Somerton whether she'd noticed anything funny going on in the billiard room, and she hooted with laughter. 'Everything about that evening was funny! The look on the faces of the staff when we took their trays off them and handed the drinkies around – and those hors d'oeuvres! I didn't think I'd stop laughing when Dilys managed to fit three of them in her mouth and did her impression of Stanley Baldwin, but that round of aspirin was the funniest thing EVER! I have NEVER been to a party and taken my hangover medicine halfway through – oh, we all did it! Although I must say, I didn't feel as bright as a summer's day the next morning. Not at all. I can't begin to imagine how much worse I'd have felt if I hadn't had it mind you – and that fabulous breakfast of course.'

'Have you ever done that before?' I asked. 'Taken medicine at a party?'

'I've no idea whose idea it was, but whoever they are should be given a medal.'

'And what did you know about Mr Cullimore?'

'Owned the paper, then passed it on to his son. Bit of a hard man, but then, perhaps one has to be if one is to succeed in business? I don't know. I saw Mr Cullimore out and about a bit. He definitely had an eye for the ladies.' She shrugged and offered me a Jaffa cake, which I gratefully accepted.

It felt like it had been a long afternoon, and I'd only been to see two of the people on the list. I left the Somerton residence, was driven back to Ampney by Baxter and, the moment I arrived, Maude told me a bath was running. Clearly, she knew what a visit to Euphemia Nash entailed, and that tea with Mrs Somerton was no picnic either.

Twenty-Five

The following morning, I wandered down to the village post office, only to find that the queue was out the shop and half way up the street. Many of the people queuing had their arms full of parcels and letters, but some had only scraps of paper in their hands – on which scant few words were written, of messages that were to be wired.

In my own case, I was there on the behest of my aunt, who had insisted I wire a Happy Birthday message to my mother in Mexico. She'd given me a pound note to cover the cost (a ludicrous amount), but she said she needed the change. I had already sent my mother a card, but it wasn't going to get there in the three days I'd allowed for it to arrive, and so here I was, standing in wait behind Mrs Anderson and her week's worth of Ampney & Wold Gazettes, that she insisted on sending to her son in Hong Kong. Did he need to know about the local artist who sketched the Spring Trees, or the names of all the new-born babies? I doubt it. I'm sure they had their own newborn babies in Hong Kong, and their own spring trees! And how did I know all of this? Because Mrs Burrows was waiting in line in front of Mrs Anderson, and she was determined to wring every bit of information out of the poor woman.

I tried to switch off my ears, and lose myself in the building's beautifully ornate stonework; its climbing ivy, its crumbling cement and the variegated dim yellow of its buttery bricks, but suddenly the name, "SHIELDS" sprang into my consciousness, and I perked up. A message seemed to have been lost or gained, because the post mistress had caught up with one of the telegram boys, and was asking him whose messages he had.

'I've got a Miss Donald, a Mr Parker, a Mrs Shields and a Mrs Peels,' he said.

'I'm Peels,' said a voice. It was a woman holding a basket full of radishes, a raincoat and an umbrella, and pushing a pram with a baby in it – and with three little girls attached, dutifully holding hands. 'It'll be from my nephew. What does it say?' she asked.

The boy held the telegram out for the woman to read, and she looked at him, pointedly. 'I don't have a hand free, sonny, would you just read it out?' at which point, the baby began crying, and one of the little girls must have done something to one of her sisters, because they suddenly began pinching and squirming.

While the young lad tore the telegram open, we all turned our heads to look away, which of course meant that our ears were directed straight at him, all the better to hear every word.

'Enjoying B water STOP Doc is fine STOP Food is lovely STOP Safe and sound STOP Missing you STOP'

'Are you sure this is for me?' she asked. 'He's not mentioned the train he's coming on.'

'Well, you told me it was yours,' said the boy, peering red-faced at the piece of paper. 'You see – Shields.'

'I'm PEELS,' she said, 'That's not my wire!'

The crowd resumed their chatter. The telegram had been of little interest, and there were murmured whispers along the lines of, "People with time to swim AND spend a bob telling other folks about it!" and "Bayswater hasn't got a dock, although it's nice enough for a dip in the summer".

Bayswater was a local lake, and it seemed like an odd thing to spend a shilling's worth of message about a picnic someone had missed. And odder still, given the rain we'd had the day before, that anyone had been dining out at all – and sent a wire to Loretta's mother about it.

By the time I'd sent my brief message to Mexico and bought a book of stamps, I was no less confused about that telegram, but I couldn't very well ask Loretta Shields' mother about it, so I returned home. There was more to this than met the eye, but I would have to get to the bottom of it by myself.

The telephone directory for our area was thicker than I'd expected. It seemed that telephones were growing in popularity and, more surprisingly, the locals were happy to be "located". I looked up *Bayswater* and found Bayswater Cycling Club, Bayswater Farm Supplies and "Bayswater, Major George, 12 Parkington Avenue, Cotswolds 8309". I gave the major a call and endured an overly long and much-repeated conversation due to the man's poor hearing, by the end of which, it was clear the major didn't swim and IF he did, he wouldn't send a telegram about it.

So, if the major wasn't the Bayswater I wanted, could it be "Bakewater"? There was no-one under the name Beakwater, Brigwater or Bakelater. Fruitless enquiries had given me a thirst, so I sloped down to the kitchen, and Cook asked me why I had a face "like a wet Wednesday"?

I told her the bits I could recall about the telegram, and she immediately launched into a conversation I only half understood. 'Break water? Ha!'

'No, no, I said "Bakewater"!'

'My word, I carried a jar of pickles around with me for a week – and that's only the beginning, of course. Hours and hours it was – just like the doc said it would be, and little Jonathan took his own sweet time, but he came in the end – unlike t'other one, who took half as long and was twice the size.'

'Are you talking about swimming?' I asked. I hadn't understood a word Cook had said since she'd started.

'Oh goodness me, no,' she said laughing and still vigorously rolling pastry at the same time. 'I'm talking about my babbers – although they're not pop-in-your-pocket little poppets now, of course. Great, huge children they are. My Jonathan's twenty-three years old, and nearly twice as tall as me and the doc says it's a miracle, given my Ernie's height!'

'I'm not sure we need to know any more about your experiences with doctors and such like, Cook,' said Maude, who'd entered with an empty teapot. 'Dinner will be late if you don't get that chicken pie in.'

Doctors?

We left the room, and I began to think about that message again – or what I remembered of it. Had it said "Bayswater" or had it been the ladies in front of me who'd started talking about that? And the food mentioned in the wire didn't have to be a picnic, of course. The "dock" could have been spelled with or without a "c", I couldn't know which without reading it, and a hospital was certainly a place that provided food. And the telegram had evidently been sent by someone who was close to Mrs Shields, in which case, spending a shilling to let someone know you were in hospital, was a lot more understandable than letting them know you'd gone swimming.

I consulted the telephone directory and looked up the local "cottage hospitals", and found three. The first was in the centre of Ampney, and when I gave the little hospital a call, I was immediately informed that if it wasn't an emergency, not to waste their time.

This was fair enough, of course, but it didn't answer any of my questions.

Twenty-Six

The following morning, I was up with the lark for some reason and, feeling rather pleased with myself, I slid into the Sunbeam's driving seat at 8.09am, after just one cup of tea.

I eased on my driving gloves, and any shadow of anxiety I might have had about owning the car that had been part of such an awful period of my life, was washed away as the engine rumbled – and all hell broke loose. Crumpet jumped in, got hold of the horn and began biting it in between barks. The diabolical din that she was making obviously enraged her and, as if that wasn't enough, Maude turned up and Crumpet began howling in between toots instead.

When the dog had finally been pulled off the horn's red bulb, Maude made it quite clear that she was unimpressed by my monastic time of day. She pointed out that if my intention was to continue enquiries with my aunt's friends, I was at least three hours too early, although I had most certainly woken everyone else up with my little performance. I returned to the house and read for a couple of hours, before joining Auntie Bathsheba for an early elevenses, and telling her about the hospital visits I was going to make.

'That all sounds marvellous,' she said. 'Oh, and about Dilly. She gave me a ring yesterday to say that she may be rather busy this coming week due to jury service. She's always happy to make up the numbers if her husband doesn't have the necessary 12, 13, however many it is, so it would be just as well to pop in and see her today *just* before lunch, not too early.'

Returning to my beautiful machine after a pot of tea, I quietly opened the door for Crumpet, and we peacefully headed down the gravel drive, off to Cerney, and the Sunbeam made what would have been a lumbering journey with Baxter, into a whiz through the countryside. When we arrived, I congratulated myself on what good time we'd made, but what we'd made up for in speed, we'd lost in length of nose, because it took ages to find a parking space bigger than an Austin 7 or a Shetland pony.

It seemed that every pub and shop in the place was having deliveries made at this hour of the day; and a reminder that, even after elevenses, mornings are too busy a time to get anything sensible done in the Cotswolds.

When Crumpet and I finally arrived at the neat, modern clinic in the centre of the village, we were overwhelmed with athletes, but there was no sign of Loretta. What were rugby players doing playing so early in the day – and during the week? As we got closer, it became apparent, that they were schoolboys – very tall ones. The "derby" had taken place between two local schools, and there were a number of broken noses. I could have stayed, waited and made enquiries, but I could see that things hadn't improved since I'd spoken with one of the nurses on the phone and, anxious to get a move on, I decided to visit my next port of call.

The next hospital on my list was in Kemble Crucis, a small town which was known for its market day – which was something I recalled twenty minutes later, when I was prevented from driving up the high street, by a herd of shaggy Cotswold sheep. Crumpet made her feelings for the sheep clear, as we attempted a twenty-point turn and the local farmers made their feelings for my motorcar and my dog clear too. After a ten-minute detour, we made it to the other end of the village, and their cottage hospital. It was an old building, with large, wibbly windows and an old brass plaque, which announced that it was the area's first cottage hospital, opened in 1868 by a local landowner, who was known as a "Royal Touch Sceptic".

(Country folk can be a bit behind the times, and this can manifest itself in wonderful ways; studiously observing the Sabbath in a quiet and respectful manner, eating fish on Fridays, throwing salt over your shoulder, etc., but it can also be less wonderful, and this was an example of the latter. The King's Touch was something that the vast majority of the population (and the King himself) had given up on over a hundred years before, and this wealthy landowner had evidently had enough of sickly locals coming to his home, demanding they be "touched" by him for healing.)

I tied Crumpet up outside and went inside, unsure of what I would find, but the hospital was clean, bright and well managed, there were no forlorn locals demanding to be cleansed or healed by my hand, and in fact, the only person present was a nurse at the desk.

'How may I help?' she asked, looking me up and down. 'You're a visitor?'

I told her she had deduced correctly, and began to say something about enquiries, when I realised that I had said the wrong thing. Looking at her clipboard, she asked me my name and then, without looking up, she told me I was not on the list. I began to explain the reason for my visit, but she held her hand up to silence me.

'You see, I've come to – to –'

Her hand remained in the air. There was no point in my speaking, so I waited for the inevitable reply.

'As I said, your name is not on the list. We are very busy, so you'll have to leave and make an appointment.'

'May I make an appointment now?' I asked, as she consulted her watch, disappeared through a doorway and I was left alone. The door had very clearly 'clicked' when she had walked through, and I wasn't likely to pick the lock of a local hospital door any time soon, so I left, picked Crumpet up outside and we wandered back to the car as the clock struck twelve. We headed back to Ampney, and our appointment with Dilys.

I'm happy to say that we managed to get a parking spot no trouble at all, when we arrived – thanks to Mr Jolly's hearse going off to the garage for a once over and, as I parked, I noticed Anthony Cullimore striding up the road. He had in his hand, a large bouquet of flowers, and so, with Crumpet under strict instructions not to make a sound, we crept along the other side of the road, many, many yards behind him – too many to be sensible, because when he walked past St John's graveyard, we lost him.

Five minutes of lurking later, and a quick tour of the graves to check that Cullimore hadn't laid the flowers at any of them, we were running late for Dilys and, if my aunt was right, the only way I'd get to see her this week, was if I were arrested and brought before her husband the judge.

Twenty-Seven

Dilys Parker had evidently been expecting me, because when I arrived, I was greeted by a beaming hostess, holding a large platter of finger sandwiches (the best in the county, apparently). Mrs Parker's home was a small cottage crammed full of things – not in the manner of Euphemia's place, I hasten to add – but the items that took pride of place, were invariably made out of knotted string. Dilys had also taken to the cocktail craze with a vengeance, and the corner of her elegant drawing room had been transformed into a cocktail bar that wouldn't have looked out of place at a funfair.

I stifled a yawn – I really had got up much too early – and unfortunately Dilys noticed, and she looked delighted! Decanting any number of colourful bottles from her cabinet, she began mixing a cocktail of her own invention, called the "Ampney Rocket".

'Isn't lunchtime a little early for spirits?' I asked, but Dilys assured me that it would add a bit of pep to my step, and cheerfully told me that she'd worked in the dispensary at the local hospital, and that she knew EXACTLY what she was doing.

And it was while she was shaking the mixture of many liquors and ice, that Dilys made clear how excited she was at the prospect of seeing her husband described in print.

'How do you know he's in Bettina's manuscript?' I asked.

'I don't, of course, and it won't be his actual name in it, but everyone will know. He's just bound to be in it. He's the local magistrate, and if you want a bit of sauce, you wouldn't leave someone like that out, would you? It would be madness!'

'And what will your husband think of that?' I asked.

She made a gesture that suggested she wasn't concerned – or that her husband couldn't read – and then presented me with something that was a dark, oily purple colour. Just the smell of it was enough to make my nostrils quiver, and I rested the glass on the chimneypiece for a moment, to give myself some space – and ask her some questions.

When I asked her about the late Mr Cullimore, her reaction was very similar to the other two women I'd spoken with. There was no love lost for the man, he had an eye for the ladies and could be a bit hard in negotiations. In fact, "an eye for the ladies", was exactly the same phrase that Mrs Somerton had used, so it seemed that everyone was agreed on this aspect of his character. I asked Dilys if she knew anything more about Mr Cullimore's relations with women.

'My grandmother said that his wife was lovely.' (Mrs Parker was no spring chicken, but what she'd said was a reminder of just how old a 102-year-old is. Cullimore had married his wife in the 1850s!) 'They had the one child – William, I think his name was, and no more after she became ill.'

'What was wrong?'

'I'm not sure. One of those illnesses that gets steadily worse... she withdrew from society entirely five or six years before the end.'

'And he didn't marry again?'

'Not that anyone knows of,' said Dilys. 'But he certainly didn't lack for female company. He had all those nurses of his, didn't he?'

After taking another sniff of my cocktail, to see if it had mellowed at all, I sidled over to a spot next to a large houseplant, before taking a taste, knowing that I had avoided the inevitable for long enough. I allowed the noxious liquid to meet my lips, and licked them, trying to stifle the cough rising up my throat. I could taste gin, vermouth and Cointreau, certainly. There was a dose of blackcurrant, a hint of... Bovril, perhaps, and something else I couldn't put my finger on.

As I managed a smile, and wondered at the sharp pain I felt behind my eyes, Dilys revealed that the secret ingredient was a home-brewed spirit made from a mixture of greengages from her garden, and a prickly pear that she'd picked up on a trip to Malta.

After tipping the whole lot into the planter while my hostess's back was turned, I thanked her for a memorable morning, and asked for directions to Amelia's house. (The Aspidistra might not survive the week, given the ingredients of the cocktail she served, but I would.)

Mrs Amelia Stewart was the oldest of the women in the Kiss & Swoon fan club by a decade or more, and she had been described by my Aunt Bathsheba, in a way that suggested she wasn't quite 'the thing' but which also suggested that she was an adequate hand at bridge, and that she had been a loyal reader and promoter of my aunt's publications. And my aunt may be a bit of a snob, but she's not a fool.

Mrs Stewart's home was a modest little terrace on the edge of the village, and when she asked me where I was staying, I told her that I was in the estate cottage, and we both agreed that the huge advantage of not living in a large home was that there wasn't too much cleaning to be done. She led me into the sitting room, which was a tight squeeze for two, and I turned a little too quickly in the small space, and caught my elbow on a figurine. By some miracle, Mrs Stewart managed to catch it, but unfortunately, she took my subsequent interest in her sideboard as an invitation to lead me into her tiny study, and show me her entire collection of porcelain. When we'd finished looking at her Limoges, I remarked – out of politeness again – that she took the Ampney & Wold Gazette. I could have kicked myself, and feared she was about to show me her collection of those as well, but her response was brief and to the point.

'Such a good read, and just as well to know what the local council are up to. It's gone right up in my estimation.' She turned to her pile of papers, and before she could begin showing me her favourite articles, I told Mrs Stewart that I had popped in to ask about the ball. When she looked a little confused, I mentioned that I thought I had seen her there, had she not attended?

'Oh, yes, yes, I was there, indeed I was. It was a very beautiful occasion, the best yet.'

'Absolutely – aside from Old Cullimore's passing -'

She let out a little yelp.

'I'm so sorry, I didn't mean to upset you, and I'm not here about that, not at all. I'm here about a missing manuscript.'

(In truth, this was the first really natural response from any of my aunt's friends about the old man's death. It was something of a relief.) 'Take a seat,' I said. 'Take your time. It was a very traumatic thing to happen, especially at a party.' Leaving her to gather her thoughts, I popped into the kitchen and put on the kettle, only to find that she'd followed me in, insisting that she do the honours; her house, her pot of tea to make. For a woman of her proportions and age, she was really very quick on her feet. I returned to her sitting room, surrounded by her ceramics, and told myself not to remark on anything in the house. I was here to ask *pertinent* questions. When Mrs Stewart walked in with the tray, she said that she hadn't stayed very long at the ball at all after what had happened, and she returned to her kitchen to fetch some digestives. I spoke to her about Bettina's missing manuscript, and she said that she tended to read Lettice's work, rather than Bettina's. And when I asked her if she'd been offered the work to read, she replied that it would probably be just as well if that particular bit of writing wasn't located.

I thanked Mrs Stewart for her time; another dead end, but a woman who had her priorities right. I got up, felt suddenly dizzy and fell back into the chair.

'Oh, you poor dear, you got up too quickly!' said Mrs Stewart, 'Low blood pressure, I shouldn't wonder. Stay right where you are.' She hurried into her kitchen and returned with a piece of chocolate, and a cold flannel which she applied to my forehead. She examined my pupils, felt my pulse and urged me to take my time.

'I'm sorry, I don't know what's come over me. Too much tea, perhaps?' I said, thinking back to the sip of cocktail I'd had with Dilys.

'Would you like me to call Dr Ferguson?' she asked. 'He's a close friend. It would be no trouble.'

'No, I'm fine, really,' I said, but Mrs Stewart looked so concerned, that I told her that my next appointment was in fact a hospital, so I'd get a once-over there.

'Nothing serious, I hope?'

I shook my head. 'No, no, it's not about me.'

'Are you visiting a friend?' she asked.

'Trying to find one, actually.'

'Well, how interesting. A young man?' And as she asked, she glanced down at the ring on my finger.

'A female friend,' I said, rising from my seat and, anxious to leave before the conversation drifted anywhere near my having a husband. I was grateful for the stiff breeze that cleared my head when Mrs Stewart opened her front door, and that was when I noticed a bouquet of flowers in her porch – the same bunch that Anthony Cullimore had been holding before I'd lost sight of him.

Mrs Stewart quickly moved me on, down the garden path, and then she walked me to the Sunbeam, waving me off as I took the Quenington road.

Twenty-Eight

The third hospital on my list, wasn't located in the middle of a town, or overwhelmed with sheep or cows, football or rugby players. And it wasn't strictly speaking, a hospital, because as soon as Crumpet and I drove onto its grounds, it became immediately obvious what the place was when I noticed the voluptuous form of most of the women there – and the number of prams. And, as if that wasn't enough, the B-Water reference in that telegram, turned out to be "Breakwater", rather than Bayswater; Cook had been right, after all.

I parked the Sunbeam and walked across the gravel, and was met by a woman wearing a pin that said "Nurse Beckett", and a uniform that was much longer, and far more "regulation" than anything Loretta had ever worn. And she didn't fill it with the kind of curves Loretta had, either.)

'This is a nursing home,' said Nurse Beckett, 'If you're seeking confinement, you've come to the right place,' she said, looking me up and down with a critical eye. 'But if you need to see a doctor, you're best off going back the way you came.' It wasn't the warmest greeting I'd ever received. I introduced myself as Georgiana Mortimer, and pointedly fiddled with my wedding ring. Now and again, my (briefly) married status added a certain weight to a situation, and when I asked if I could see Loretta Shields, the nurse consulted a clipboard and asked if I was on the list. I had to admit I wasn't, so she said she would check with the patient – and then told me that there was nobody staying at Breakwater by that name.

But I was sure Loretta was here. There was no sign of her at the tavern or the château – and the librarian, Mrs Burrows, said she hadn't been seen in weeks. "The butler at Old Cullimore's, said she'd gone to see a sister on the coast. What sister? She wasn't a woman with a sister, anyone can tell the sort -" And so it went on.

If Loretta wasn't on their list, it didn't of course mean she wasn't staying here. What alternate name might she use – or might the person who was paying for this rather swanky establishment, have suggested? I thought back to what Peter had whispered to himself, about her being a goddess, and tentatively tried 'Helen Troy?'

'No.'

'Venus D. Milo?'

'No, Mrs Mortimer.'

'Cleopatra...' I said, struggling to think what the Egyptian queen's surname might have been, before realising she hadn't actually been a deity, but Nurse Beckett had already lost patience with me. And that was before Crumpet ran off, barking.

'PLEASE, will you sort out your dog, Mrs Mortimer. In fact, I think it might be time for you to leave. The care of our ladies is our top priority, and a barking dog is not conducive to the rest and relaxation of...'

Her words rang in my ears as I ran out of the lobby and round the side of the building, following the dog's frenzied barking, which had stopped – and been replaced by howls. And

I was running so fast, I almost ran into the little dog, when she ran back in my direction, and then turned on a sixpence, back around the corner from which she'd come. 'What is it, Crummy?' And the words were no sooner out of my mouth, than I came upon a woman lying on the grass. She was a funny colour, breathing deeply and covered in a sheen of sweat.

'I'm going to get help, Crum. You stay here and look after her. STAY.'

I sprinted back around to the nurse, and she called to her colleagues to get a wheelchair, and ran with me to the woman on the ground. We were soon surrounded by a busy and professional team of nurses, who whisked her away and, left breathless by the incident, Crumpet and I sat on a bench in the grounds, unsure what to do.

Twenty minutes later, the Nurse Beckett returned to us, to say that the young woman was delivered of a healthy daughter – and that there was one more Georgiana in the world!

I was brought a cup of tea, and allowed to visit my new namesake, which was highly irregular, according to Matron, who was no more enamoured of me than Nurse Beckett had been when I'd arrived, but the needs of the new mother came first. And there was no doubt in any of our minds that Crumpet had heard the woman's cry of distress, when nobody else had.

'Georgie?'

I turned to see a young woman with blonde curls, and an engaging smile that I recognised.

'Loret-'

'Fancy meeting you here!' she said, quickly.

'Bet you didn't think you'd meet Enid in a place like this,' she said and, as Loretta linked her arm in mine, I had to agree.

We were approached by Nurse Beckett, who asked, 'Am I to understand that you know this visitor, Enid?'

'I do, yes.'

'Right. Well in that case, there's a pot of tea in the dining room, if you want it, but the dog must stay in the car.' And with that, she left us to it. 'Seems a little ungrateful after everything you've done this afternoon,' I told Crumpet, 'But perhaps a cottage hospital isn't quite the right place for you.'

It was only when we'd poured our tea and were heading towards a table and chairs, that I had a chance to have a good look at Loretta, and noticed how much less round she was than the other women here.

'Enid?' I asked.

'Loretta is my middle name and Shields is the name of my mam's second husband. It's my stage name,' she said, blushing. 'Actually, I'm registered as Enid Rowbotham.'

I nodded in understanding. I'd have changed my name too, if it had been Enid Rowbotham, besides which, Loretta Shields suited her very well. 'It looks to me like you'll be here a while longer than some of the ladies,' I said.

'Yes,' she said with a hearty laugh, and taking a generous bite of an iced bun. 'I'm here for a few more months,' she said. 'But it's a nice spot to be, and it beats being on my feet all day, pulling pints at the Red Lion.'

'And is this why you didn't go to the wake?' I asked.

'Not really. I mean, I wanted to, of course. But there were problems with that. It didn't feel safe.'

I asked her what she meant, and she told me that there was somebody out there who wasn't a particular fan of hers, and when I pressed her for details, all she would say was that she'd received a couple of nasty letters; and no, she hadn't kept them.

'This is none of my business,' I said, 'but... are you married?'

'Any day now, and hopefully not too late,' she said with a shy smile, stroking her tummy. 'We're going up to Scotland, so that we don't have to post the banns. And anyway, there's a chance that... that someone will stand up and object if we do it in a church. The local barmaid isn't the *lady* they had in mind for him,' she said carefully, avoiding any names.

'That's wonderful,' I said. 'I do have just one more question. When we spoke at the Red Lion, I asked who you'd been with before Mr Cullimore died, and you wouldn't say. I just wondered where you got that spot of blood from?'

'Blood?'

'There was blood on your uniform.'

She looked genuinely baffled, and then her face cleared. 'Oh! That was that man! He bumped into me when I was walking through the house, and said he needed medical attention. I suppose he saw my uniform and thought I could help.'

'Who was he, do you know?'

'I gave him a napkin. It was my first real bit of nursing,' she said, beaming. 'But I've no idea who he was. He'd come in from the garden and said he'd had "a spot of bother with a door" but I've worked as a barmaid long enough that I know when someone's been punched on the nose.'

As I'm sure you recall, aside from my strange encounter with a mysterious man in the stables, I had had a rather more energetic encounter with Roger Elton; the man on whom I had practised my *suffrajitsu* on Ampney's lawn. And it sounded very like Roger was the man Loretta had bumped into, in which case, I was the "spot of bother" that he'd encountered.

I picked up my bag, and I was about to leave, when I remembered another question – another last question, I had to ask. 'Do you have a sister, Loretta?'

Annoyingly she said no. Mrs Burrows was right.

'VISITING HOURS ARE OVER, THE LADIES HAVE TO REST. PUT YOUR FLOWERS AWAY, MADAM – BRING THEM NEXT WEEK. OFF YOU GO. EVERYONE OUT!' The voice of Nurse Beckett rang in our ears, and I was the first to be ushered outside.

I was still none the wiser as to who Loretta had spent time with in the Ampney Orangery. And I wondered whether the mystery man had thought she was a real nurse, and she had been lured away to leave Old Frank Cullimore unprotected.

Twenty-Nine

Escorting me out of the building and into my car, I asked Nurse Beckett how long she expected the young woman to stay.

'As long as it takes,' she said, 'There is never a set date with these things, Mother Nature doesn't use a watch.'

'But she doesn't look like she's very far along. Is it usual to arrive as early as this – if you're healthy, I mean?'

'It is a little unusual from that point of view,' she admitted. 'But for a lot of ladies, it's also a question of cost.'

Crumpet jumped into the seat next to me, and I leaned across and closed the door. Before starting the engine, I looked up at the house again, and admired its modern, clean lines and its generous parkland setting; this was definitely costing someone a small fortune, and I thought about what Loretta has said about feeling threatened.

Getting away was more difficult than parking had been – several visitors had arrived, and my Sunbeam was packed between a Bentley and a Daimler. And anxious as I was not to scratch my car, I was even more anxious about scratching one of theirs, and I was grateful for the three nurses who insisted on giving me instructions as I reversed.

I drove out of the grounds, turned onto the Cirencester Road and headed home. The sun was trying to shine, it wasn't too cold, and I didn't think we were eating liver tonight. Everything was right with the world. The road was a quiet one with hedgerows on either side, but, within a minute or so, I was surprised to find myself boxed in by a couple of cars; the one in front going dreadfully slowly, and the one behind pushing me on.

The car in front eventually turned off in the direction of Bristol, but the one behind stayed where it was; firmly glued to my bumper. I sped up and it sped up, I slowed down and quickly sped up again – trying to give the car the hint, but it evidently had no intention of slowing down, or pulling away. The road was clear, and there were several points it could overtake, but it didn't – and the road was getting narrower. Looking in the mirror, I couldn't see the driver hounding me, the afternoon sun was shining in my eyes and on their windscreen.

I carried on speeding, getting faster and faster with every corner. Clipping hedges and skidding on gravel, the sound of screeching metal as branches scratched at the car's doors and windows.

Daring to look away from the road, I glanced down at Crumpet, who was in the footwell, looking up at me with big, fearful eyes. If I could have joined the little dog down there, I would have done, but I was struggling to stay in control on the road from hell, with a devil of a driver behind me, and a junction to a busy road coming up. I tried to flex my fingers, because my grip on the wheel had become painful, but I daren't let go.

I could see the road ahead, and how busy it was, and I had two options. Slow down, or speed up. I touched the brake lightly, and felt a violent jolt as the car behind nudged me onwards. All I could do was speed up.

'Crumpet my darling,' I said through gritted teeth, 'Time to hold on!' I closed my eyes, saw a small break in the traffic, honked the horn, gripped the wheel and looked straight ahead through half-closed eyes. We made it across – almost – until my rear was nudged by a car in the second lane, and we careered into a hedge.

The car that had clipped me, sped past, apparently untouched, but the same could not be said about my beautiful Sunbeam. I fell out of the driver's seat onto the grass, got to my feet and burned my hand on the bonnet as I propped it open to let the steam out. The front bumper was dented and there were scratches down its sides, but as far as I could tell, the front axle was straight.

By the time the local police came, I had stopped feeling angry, and started shaking instead. Crumpet was still curled up in the footwell, and seemed to be suffering from some level of shock as well. She was licking my fingers for comfort – but she managed a growl when the constable looked in on her, and I realised it was Routledge. With a wearied sigh, he asked me what had happened, and I told him as much as I could, although I realised that the details were hazy – not least because I had a cut on my temple that was beginning to hurt, and I didn't want it dripping on Louise's Schiaparelli knitwear (two seasons old, but still...).

'When did this occur, Mrs Mortimer?' he asked, taking notes.

'Thirty minutes ago. And it would have been less if you'd got here sooner.'

'Where exactly did this happen?'

'Where we're standing now, as you can plainly see. I didn't crash somewhere over there and push my wreck of a car over to this hedge.'

'What make of car was it, that you allege pushed you across the junction?'

'I have absolutely no idea, and there's no "allege" about it!'

'What colour was the car?'

'A dark colour – just like all the cars passing and, before you ask, I didn't notice how many headlights it had, or whether they were working.'

'Right. Can you tell me anything at all about the car?'

'It was big. Big enough to push me into the traffic,' I said, 'And it's a miracle I survived. The sun was in my eyes, so I couldn't see very much of it, but somebody must have!'

'And what did the driver look like?' (I glared at him, and he rephrased it with a bored tone.) 'Is there anything at all you can tell me about him, Mrs Mortimer?'

'He might have been... wearing goggles? It was hard to tell.'

'But you said earlier that it wasn't an open-top car.'

I nodded and my head hurt. It had just begun to rain.

'So, to sum up, you were bumped into by a dark-coloured car that there is no sign of, by someone you don't recognise and could not identify – except for the possibility of goggles – and by a car that left no marks to speak of on the back of your own.' The man took a peek at the bumper again, and I looked again too, and had to agree that there were bumps and scratches, but nothing that suggested what I'd experienced. The Sunbeam was too well made.

'And you state that the sun was in your eyes and impeded your vision,' said Inspector Routledge, closing his notebook.

'Correct,' I said, relieved that the nightmare was over – and then concerned by his pause.

'We have no witnesses to a second vehicle,' he went on. 'Is there any question that you didn't see the junction due to the sun?'

I harrumphed at that.

'Or did you, by any chance, enjoy a glass of sherry with your lunch?'

'I haven't eaten a thing!' I said, 'Let alone drunk anything.'

'Do you drive erratically when hungry?' he asked.

'I -' There was nothing more to be said, clearly.

'Mr Evans here will tow your car away, but in future, it might be an idea to take things more slowly. This could have been a very nasty accident, and we're lucky no-one was seriously injured.'

I pointed at my head, which was throbbing, but the policeman left, and Crumpet and I were invited to take a seat in Mr Evan's tow truck.

The inspector had asked a lot of questions, and found out very little, admittedly; but the one question he hadn't asked was why somebody would want to drive me off the road, and endanger my life.

If I wasn't very careful, I'd be joining Old Mr Cullimore in the graveyard.

Thirty

I woke up with a tearing headache, aching limbs and a black eye, none of which was a surprise. I finally managed to get up and get dressed and I joined my aunt on the terrace for a pot of tea and bacon and eggs. Baxter had been kind enough to take Crumpet off to the garage (the one run by his son), because the small dog's usual levels of empathy had been missing that morning. She'd spotted a rabbit in the grounds at half past seven, and when she'd started barking, I'd thought my head was going to fall off.

When I told my aunt about my little incident on the road, she told me that I really didn't have to continue with my enquiries if I didn't want to. 'If the police dig up my mother-in-law's garden, then I shall just replant it with something else. Something cheery like daffodils.'

She had attempted to make me feel better, but my aunt's hatred of daffodils was legendary, and if she so much as got a sniff of one on the grounds, she would demand that it be dug up and burned that very day. Aunt Sheba may not be a country woman, but she has strong feelings about her flowerbeds. I told her that I was happy to continue – all the more so since I had to find out who had wanted me off the road, and she smiled serenely. My answer had been the right one.

I got up, intending to go for a stroll around the grounds, to help heal my poor, pounding head, when the balmy silence was pierced by cackling.

'Who is that?' I asked with a grimace.

'Oh, that'll be the Girls,' said my aunt. 'They don't want to write in town until the roof is fixed, although I'm sure the townhouse is more than habitable by now, but they're fidgety and bored here.' My aunt's almost constant enquiries as to the state of her home in Pimlico were clear indications that she'd had enough of the countryside, and of restless writers.

'Isn't there anywhere else they can go?' I asked, stroking my temples.

'Don't mind them,' said my aunt, 'They're off to the spa this afternoon. You could join them if you like.'

'Oh, really? But I've still got appointments to see a few of your friends,' I said.

'In which case the Girls can wait until you're free,' said my aunt. 'Madame Beaufort is running a special, you can get a massage and a manicure for half price. Go with them when you're done with your questions. My treat, after everything you've been up to. And perhaps throw in a facial as well. We want those bruises to go down, and your beauty regime doubtless suffered while you were inside.'

She was right, of course, Holloway Prison wasn't the beauty break I had hoped it would be, unless having someone reshape your nose was top of your agenda.

My head was still pounding, so I returned to my bed for a little nap – just half an hour – and I woke up determined to seize the rest of the day. I rose, and a pot of tea and a plate of garibaldis helped, as did a couple of aspirin, but when Maude saw the colour of my cheeks, they were closely followed by a dose of soda-mint. And when Auntie Bathsheba said she was popping upstairs to find her bismuth, and Cookie said she'd make me a bone broth, I made my excuses and rushed out of doors, found the gardener's bicycle and escaped for an hour of fresh air.

It was a cool morning, the sky was that keen, bright blue so reminiscent of the Alps, and everything smelled grassy. My thighs were thankful for the exercise and when I was half way round the estate wall, I stopped, lay the bike down, and slowly and carefully climbed up a tree.

The days were getting lighter and warmer, and it wasn't just the robins singing any more.

The view was lovely; a leafy, shadowed lane on one side, and the estate on the other. The cherry tree grove was in full bloom, and the haze of soft, pink petals and the lush green grass was a sight for sore eyes. I realised I hadn't taken the time to appreciate my surroundings – or my freedom – since being released. And I thought of the women I knew in Holloway, who wouldn't see the cherry, apple or pear blossom. The prison garden was always a sight for sore eyes, but more practical in nature; nothing was being grown that couldn't be added to a potato soup or served with liver. Did Marjorie miss her biscuit-eating companion at midnight? Was anyone telling Ivy stories at bedtime – or was she reading her own?

And as I pondered the fate of the women "inside" – and wondered about the path my own liberty would take me, I heard the distant sound of horse's hooves, and saw a rider come up over the brow of the hill. He rode like he'd been born on a horse, and with loose hands and a relaxed seat, he jumped Hobb's Hedge like a professional. It was an impressive sight, and I wondered idly whether I'd seen him before – or his silhouette perhaps, and much as I would have liked to have jumped on my bike and followed him, the rider was long gone, and it was a long way down to my rickety old bicycle. (Oh, do calm down, Georgie!)

Stretching out my aching arms, I let a long sigh ring out and noticed streaks of white blossom on one of my sleeves. It reminded me of billiard chalk – of the billiard chalk that Anthony Cullimore had used, and I wondered why French chalk wasn't greeny-blue like ours. And then I wondered whether there was a young French woman sitting half-way up a tree, somewhere across the channel, watching a distant rider, telling herself to calm down, and wondering why everyone else's billiard chalk wasn't white... Jack had certainly made a point to the young policeman when she'd snorted up a line of chalk from the baize of the billiard table, which reminded me that there was more than one way to administer a drug. It could be taken up the nose, dissolved in champagne, taken with a glass of water or injected into a vein.

The assumption was that Old Cullimore had drunk the cyanide that killed him, but what if he'd ingested it some other way? What was it Dr Ferguson had said? His entire body had been checked over and, for a man his age, he was in remarkably good condition. The odd bruise on his shins and one on his foot, but otherwise, very well indeed (or at least, he had been until his evening in the billiard room.)

And I wondered whether Jack had finished that cue she was working on.

I shifted my position and felt the rough bark against the back of my legs, and suddenly remembered that I was wearing my aunt's daughter-in-law's jodhpurs. Louise was definitely not a woman given to climbing trees on a whim, so I took one, long, last breath of the fresh, beautiful air in amongst the elm leaves and gingerly climbed back down, hoping not to catch any threads.

By the time I returned to the house, both Bathsheba and Cook agreed that my rosy cheeks were the result of bismuth and broth (neither of which I'd partaken of) and I was granted a perfectly normal, non-invalid, lunch. (A glass of lemonade and a cheese and pickle sandwich on the terrace, if you must know. A vintage cheddar with a delicious tang, and Maude's home-made pickle. An absolute delight and a now-proven cure for a headache.)

Thirty-One

I had a little time before lunch, so I made a call. Dr Ferguson is a tricky man to track down, and after speaking with the man's wife, his secretary, and five ailing households, the young girl on the switchboard got hold of him at the household of a family suffering from vertigo.

'Ferguson speaking.'

'Oh, hullo, this is just a quick call -'

'I should think so! I'm on a call, you know, I've got people falling over left, right and centre!'

'Yes, I'm sorry about that. It's Georgie Mortimer, Lawrence Godfrey's niece-'

'Ah, the Honourable Godfrey... Mrs Mortimer you say? Well, how nice to hear from you. How can I help?'

I heard a thud in the background and decided to keep my call quick. 'You mentioned that Cullimore had a bruise on his foot. Can you describe it?'

'Distinctly circular and blue.'

'Blue? Doesn't that mean it's fairly fresh?' I asked.

'It does – oh – I really ought to go now!'

I thanked him, ended the call, and went in search of Jack. Peter and Anthony were still in my sights, and I had a theory about Cullimore's death, that I was anxious to discuss.

When she was on the house grounds, Jack could reliably be found in one of three places; the kitchen, the stables or the coach house, and when she wasn't at Ampney, she was at the pub. When and where she did her writing, I had no idea, although on the rare occasion she was in the Writing Room at the townhouse, she spent a great deal of time tinkering with the mechanics of her typewriter.

On this occasion, she was in the stables, helping to comb the horses' manes, and I asked her about the cue she'd been working on.

'It's going very well!' she said, marching towards the coach house. 'Oh, no, it isn't there. Come along, Georgie!' I followed her into the house, and into the billiard room where I found the usual small cue, and a cue the like of which I'd never seen. What was particularly interesting about it, was that it wasn't entirely straight. (Most of them are.) It had a strange kink in the middle – the section that had been added to make it the requisite five feet long, according to Jack.

Jack took the red and the white balls, placed them on the table, and took a shot which very nearly ripped the baize. 'Haven't got my eye in yet,' she said, squinting. 'I'll have another go at that later, although it could be a problem with the weight of it.'

'I was wondering... a cue made out of three different bits – or however many it's supposed to be – would it be possible do you think to, um add, a little something at the end that could...'

'Oh, spit it out, Georgie! What is it you want to say?'

I took a deep breath, and started again. 'Could a cue be made that could administer a drug to someone if the end of it were poked into them?'

Jack took the suggestion a lot more calmly – and seriously – than most people would, and while she gave it some thought, I in turn, considered how I might make it into Anthony Cullimore's home to check the contents of his cue case. Or perhaps I'd have to go back to the newspaper offices; maybe that was where he hid it. Or would it be easier to challenge the man to a game, and check his cue while he went for a pint? Or might he come here for an afternoon's play? My thoughts were interrupted, by a very positive 'mm' sound from Jack, who had untwisted her own mangled cue into its constituent pieces and was peering at the screws.

'What are you thinking?' I asked.

'Well, one might for example, run a line all the way down the centre of the butt, which is the end piece – behind where the screw is here – a tube or pipe down which poison might be fed. You could, if you handled it very carefully, fit a pin into the bumper at the end to prick the skin and leave a trace of something, although as a player you'd have to be very careful you didn't catch your own leg or foot, or that you didn't knock the pin head off.'

'But would it be possible?' I asked.

'Oh, it would be possible all right. You're thinking of Old Cullimore, are you?'

'Yes, you see, you mentioned the fuss about the cue landing on his foot, and I've just spoken with Dr Ferguson and he confirmed that the man had a circular bruise on the top of his foot. And it being blue signifies, obviously, that the bruising happened before he died, and that it was done recently.'

'Ah, yes, there was a bit of a fuss,' said Jack, screwing her cue back together again.

'Really? Could the poison have been administered then?' I asked, grateful that she was still taking my suggestion so seriously. 'Could Anthony Cullimore have somehow added some element or contraption to the end of his cue so that when it dropped onto his great grandfather's foot, it gave him a dose of something fatal?'

'Absolutely,' she said. 'Without a doubt. Only, I was the one who dropped the cue on Cullimore's foot, not Tony.'

'Ah.'

'And before you ask, Georgie, the stuff I snorted up off the baize, in front of that constable, was chalk. Just chalk.'

Oh. Back to the drawing board. The subject was dropped and I was grateful when Jack suggested a quick game of billiards.

We hit our balls, and it was decided that mine was closest to the baulk head, so I would start. The red was set on the billiard spot, I placed my cue ball in the D and I broke first. When it was Jack's turn to play, she made a break of four hundred and something, and it was a relief when lunch was announced. It seemed she'd got the hang of her wonky old cue after all.

Thirty-Two

I returned to my manuscript enquiries in the afternoon, and Baxter was kind enough to do the honours, although I suspect a part of that was how much he enjoys driving the Sunbeam.

Kiss & Swoon fan club member, Fiona Tolliver, lived in a curiously circular cottage in the middle of the village, in an almost circular plot – with a dreadfully squeaky gate, as a result of which, she was standing at the front door when I arrived. Her home was expensively and tastefully furnished, all of the fittings curved to fit the walls. I introduced myself and remarked on how lovely her home was – which wasn't just blithe politeness. If I'd lived in Ampney Tet, I would have wanted to live in a home like hers, although I know that in actual fact, my taste would have been off in a number of areas, and my love of colour would have marred the elegant put-together nature of her home.

Even if some of the décor was fraying at the edges, were one giving out points for design, Mrs Tolliver's home was a firm nine out of ten, although the same could not be said of her clothing. Fiona was firmly floral, from head to toe. She wore shoes with appliquéd flowers on them, a dress and cardigan that were floral, a bracelet adorned with cloisonné roses, and a velvet sunflower in her hair.

After the usual pleasantries, Mrs Tolliver complimented me on my jewellery and I realised that I was wearing daisy pearl earrings and a Liberty's blossom print blouse as well. Oh, how dreadful!

As she put the kettle on, I asked if her husband was at work, and after a moment of confusion, she blushed and told me that Mr Tolliver was her brother.

'Oh…' I said, and, anxious to change the topic of conversation, I told "Mrs" Tolliver, that I had come round to ask about the missing manuscript. Fiona primly assured me that she was only a reader of Lettice's work, rather than Bettina's, and that she'd only heard about the manuscript, but hadn't seen it – and that she wasn't sure it was "quite her cup of tea". (And I wondered how many of my aunt's readers only ever admitted to reading Lettice's work.)

'Of course, it was a shock the day after the ball,' she said, 'When I heard Bettina's work had gone missing, because your aunt had offered me a peek of it at that rather jolly breakfast before the hunt. Bathsheba says my spelling is better than Bettina's.'

'She offered to show it to you at the breakfast?' I asked, surprised that the lady had made it all the way through to eight in the morning – and thinking there must be some confusion. So, I then asked Mrs Tolliver about the demise of Mr Cullimore – to see how much of that story she had straight, and whether sleep deprivation might play a part in her recollections.

'Well, let me see, there was a group of us in the billiard room, all enjoying the music, well, *some* of the music – and having a nice old natter, you know. The drinks were flowing, there were such delicate pastries to be had. I must say, your aunt holds such wonderful occasions – and it was all very jolly and suddenly there was all this hullabaloo! Although, it didn't last long. The music, the *nice* music, began again soon enough.'

'And Mr Cullimore?'

'Mm, poisoned at that age, well, it seems like a waste of resources if you ask me. Another cup?' she asked, brightly.

Had I heard her right? I declined the cup of chamomile, and asked 'Did you like Mr Cullimore?' – at which point she took a long, long sip of her tea.

'Goodness me, I couldn't say, only, well, his attitude towards young Anthony has been unforgivable.'

'His grandson? What did he do to him?'

'Oh, it's not for me to say. It's all water under the bridge and firmly resolved now... another cup of chamomile?'

The image I had formed of Old Cullimore, was being shattered with every conversation that I had, although nothing very definite was being said; and the image I had of my aunt's friends (or at least, of her readers) was being shattered too. What exactly had Old Cullimore done, that so few villagers were sad or even shocked that he had been murdered?

Desperate for a "proper" cup of tea, Baxter took me round to the home of Elizabeth Hampshire. She and my aunt were close chums; they spent similar amounts of time in town, which they regarded as their natural habitat, and their boys were the same sort of age. I had heard my aunt refer to her friend, Lizzy's home as a "cottage" but there was nothing twee or diminutive about it. Charming, yes, but enormous, and located on extensive grounds, it was a far cry from Amelia's modest home, Euphemia's overgrown hideaway, Dilys' macramé and cocktails or Honoria's head-turning art. (And still, it was a fraction of the size of my aunt and uncle's place.)

I asked after the lady of the house, and was told by a young maid that she was holidaying in Wales and would return to Ampney in a week's time, at which point another maid asked me my name, nodded and then asked me to wait. She put through a call to a number in Pembroke.

'Yes, madam, Lady Bathsheba's niece is here... Is she here about the manuscript? I'll ask.'

I informed her that I was.

'Yes, madam, she says she is... you'll take a morning train in... three days' time... one thirty? Yes, I've made a note of it... no, he isn't free tomorrow, but he says he can fit you in next week... yes, they have been fed... no, it is still broken... right, madam, thank you, I shall be sure to tell her.'

So, it seemed that this friend of Bathsheba's was willing to cut a holiday in half and jump on a train, three days' early, in order to assist in my enquiries. Was this the action of a guilty party, I wondered? I would return later in the week.

Thirty-Three

Feeling enlivened and, with no one to question, I told my aunt that a trip to the spa would be just the thing.

Bettina, Jack and Lettice were delighted, and at two o'clock, the four of us jumped in the Bentley with Baxter – and Crumpet, who needed some fresh air. My aunt was convinced that Crummy was still suffering from the shock of the crash, and she needed some tender loving care. It could also have been that Maude had had enough of the little dog.

The spa my aunt had booked, was called Greenland Manor; a stately home whose owners had had to sell up due to tax difficulties, which had been bought by Madam Beaufort and renamed Beaufort House. As her name suggests, the woman in charge was French and, like so many of her countrywomen, a firm believer that *all women are beautiful*, regardless of age, shape or size, and can only be made more so by the judicious application of cream, running water, scented oils and a firm, Hungarian hand.

Aesthetically, the manor was interesting, and a far cry from every other stately home I've ever visited. The really expensive part of owning such a property had been overcome by Madam

B bringing all the outdoor statues indoors – as examples of classical beauty – and the stone benches had come in too, thereby negating the need for costly furnishings.

Where previously, tapestries had been displayed, and Jacobean wood panelling had adorned the walls, white curtains now hung – and doubtless kept out any draughts. But given the sheer scale of the place, I couldn't imagine how it was kept as warm as it was.

The silent, serious-faced staff striding about with armfuls of thick, fluffy towels all added to the air of professionalism and, as soon as I arrived, my aching head was a distant memory.

Lime, rosemary and jasmine filled the air, along with the distant sound of harp playing, and I craned to see if it were a gramophone or a local music student, but could see no evidence of either.

The four of us changed into towelling robes and slippers, and we were taken to the *Salle d'Eau*, where we were showered with high pressure hoses, slathered with soap, violently brushed and showered down again, before our robes were returned to us. (Of course, I say that, but the robe I was given had a pipe in the pocket – which I handed to Jack.) Feeling tired and a bit shocked, it was a pleasure to be led into the treatment room, where we were invited to lie down, and our faces were cleansed, massaged, clayed, baked, recleansed, steamed, creamed, oiled, massaged, wiped and creamed again. And the last stage of our treatment was a warm foot spa, whilst wrapped in an extra towel with slices of cucumber over our eyes. It was bliss.

After half an hour of foot care and a wonderfully enlivening massage (by the silent and powerful György, whose hands looked like they could have wrestled bulls) – my companions and I were granted half an hour's nap, to the sounds of the mysterious harp. We returned to the changing room and did our best to put our clothes back on – with pleasure-addled fingers and oiled legs that made the application of stockings perilous. And from there? We stumbled straight into the orangery for afternoon tea.

It was perhaps the only part of the place that had been mostly left in its original state, and we were brought two pots of tea, a plate of fruit tarts and a bottle of champagne.

The four of us sat in silence, glowing.

It had been a calm, lovely afternoon, and my bruises from the accident were grateful for the care they'd received – the beauticians had drawn straws to see who would have to deal with me. Looking through the high, arched windows, we watched a herd of deer run by, rapidly followed by a small, barking dog, an elderly chauffeur and a Hungarian masseur.

I was glad to see that Crumpet had got over any trauma she'd suffered from the car accident, and relieved when they caught up with her, before she caught up with the deer.

Turning away from the tableau outside, I admired the room's frescos; a mural showed the muses; each of them holding something that illustrated their particular art, and showed off their glowing limbs. The goddesses' cheeks were rosy enough that they looked like they had just undergone the spa's showering treatment, and one of them in particular, caught my eye.

She was a woman with her back to us, glancing over her shoulder with coy invitation, her Titian hair flowing in luscious curls across her shoulders, bright sparkling eyes, a dimple in her chin. Could it... no! It couldn't be, could it? It was. It was a painting of Loretta Shields. She held in her hand, a lyre, while a chubby little baby sat at her feet.

'Which of the muses is that one?' I asked the ladies. I knew the muse of dance was Terpsichore, but that was the extent of my knowledge.

'It's Euterpe, the muse of music,' said Lettice with confidence.

'No,' said Bettina, 'I don't think so. Euterpe is holding the flute – she's the figure over there. The one Georgie's pointing at is Erato.'

'How can you tell which is which?' asked Lettice.

'The cherub is Eros,' said Bettina. 'Erato is the muse of love poetry.'

I wandered over to the far corner of the mural, but I could find no artist's name.

While the ladies finished their afternoon tea, I went to the front desk and asked if I could speak with Madame Beaufort, and I told the receptionist I wanted to discuss the art on display, and she seemed to approve.

I was shown through a door to a small room at the back of the spa and, unlike the rest of the house, this little room was firmly traditional. No white, silver or marble to be seen. A lush Persian carpet covered the floor, tapestries covered the walls and Madame Beaufort was seated in a large, dimpled, red leather armchair, at a wide, mahogany desk which was covered in stains. I could only guess that they were something to do with the bunches of dried lavender, sage, rosemary (and other herbs and flowers I didn't recognise) and the half a dozen bottles of oil that covered it.

And the woman herself? Madame Beaufort was in her early sixties, at a guess. Her face was well lived in, but cared for, she was slim, lively and sat with a back that was ramrod straight. Her lipstick was magenta and perfectly complemented her navy-blue wool dress.

'I 'op you 'ave 'ad a pleasant stay?' she asked, although I could see that she was puzzled by the pale purple skin around my eyes.

'I 'ave – have – indeed, I have – and I feel much better than I did when I arrived,' I assured her. 'Actually, what I am here to ask about is the mural in the orangery? ... the muses on the wall?'

'Yes!' She clapped her hands together. 'A wonderful work zat we commissioned from an up and comeeng *artiste* 'oo 'as made it quite lovely. Some of ze ladies 'e painted are regulars' of ours who were privileged to be included, and *à mon avis*, it makes a little jollity. Beautiful women in a beautiful place.'

'Yes, absolutely. I just wondered who the artist is? It isn't signed.'

'Adlington is 'is name, and if you can get 'old of one, you must. 'is pieces are ... *chers maintenant*,' she said, and she rubbed her fingers together to show just how pricey Leo's art was now. I thanked her for the information, and returned to my champagne.

So, it seemed that Adlington's sketch of Loretta had been more than a one-off, and he had chosen her to be his love goddess.

And I wondered whether Adlington's art was making enough now, that he could pay for a long stay at the Breakwater Cottage Hospital.

Thirty-Four

I told my aunt what I'd seen on the walls of Beaufort, and that I was considering jumping on the train back up to Mayfair the next day, to ask Adlington some questions.

'He won't be there,' she said.

'How do you know?'

'Because of the Wickbury Art Festival, my dear.'

'There's an arts festival?'

'*Art*, not arts. No dancing, singing or acrobats. Art in Wickbury; some of it fine, some of it less so, but the festival happens every single year, without fail. I can't quite believe you've missed it.' She peered at me in a way that suggested that – just for a moment – she thought I was demented.

'You're not talking about the Flower Festival, are you?'

She gave that some thought. 'Ah, yes. You see, it began as a Flower Festival, and then the arty bit got too big.'

'And is this something they've done in the last five years?' I asked, 'Since I moved to London?'

'You may have a point, yes.' She took a sip of her tea. 'Anyway, there is an Art Festival and it's quite something. It's Dilys who arranges it and gets all the artists and dealers on board – and Freddy, who I think you've met?'

If Dilys was involved, it was bound to be interesting, and as I reached for my tea, Maude placed a leaflet on the table.

The Wickbury Art Festival - *"The Pride of the Cotswolds."*
A chance to see artists from near and far, interpret the beautiful Cotswolds landscape, its products and its people, in oil, ink, watercolour and string.
Included in this year's line-up, are Sir Denham Moorcroft, Lydia Avery, Quentin Smith, Leo Adlington, Thomas Tingle, Christine Hunter, Thomas Bowers and others.
Friday at 2pm. *A talk will be given on the subject of 'The Colours of the Cotswolds: Can Justice be done to a Landscape rendered in Ink?' by Thomas Tingle*
Friday at 5pm. *Still Life: Just a Dead Fish on a Plate. Discuss. T. Bowers.*
Saturday at 11am. *Knot a Waste of Time – Have a Go at Macramé!*
Saturday at 2pm. *Quentin Smith will be signing copies of his latest book,*
'Beyond the Eye – A Life in Watercolour'.
Saturday at 3.30pm. *When does a Portrait become a Caricature? A look at the Work of Sir Eustace Pevney (1828 – 1897).*
Saturday at 5pm. *Prize-giving and Student Bursary Award (n.b. These awards are for artists, not artistes.)*
Sunday – *General Sale Day and Closing Ceremony.*

'Do I have to buy a ticket for any of this?' I asked.

'Heavens no,' said my aunt. 'The more the merrier, as far as Dilys is concerned, although Freddy tends to take it a little more seriously. The committee voted in favour of tickets two years ago, and the art sales revenue fell by 35%, and at one of the talks given, there were more people on the stage than there were in the audience.'

'What was the talk about?' I asked.

'Something to do with string, I think.'

Mindful of the fact that I would have to return to the real world sooner or later, I spent the following morning, writing application letters to all the magazines I knew. My uncle had run up a short list of publications for me – mostly of people that he knew at the Paternoster Club, but on the unspoken agreement that I wouldn't mention our connection. I wrote to my old place of work, *Domestic Bliss*, just for good measure, but I didn't expect very much back. *Just in Time* was a magazine about jewellery and watches, and they were always looking for people to write for them, and I applied despite my lack of horological knowledge. It was worth a try, surely? I sent my CV to *Blooming Lovely, My Home Journal, The Covent Garden Gazette, Frivolous Fitzrovia, Champagne and Silk* (I wasn't quite sure what that was), *Vogue, The Queen, Tatler* (of course) and *Soho Scene*, amongst others.

The question was whether anyone would know that Miss Georgie Wren had got married; given that employing married women was a no-no. Or that they would be aware that "Mrs Georgiana Mortimer", a widow – and therefore employable, had spent time in prison – making her much less employable. In fact, more of a NO than a mere no-no.

Wondering whether any of them would be familiar with "Miss" G. Mortimer, I signed the letters accordingly.

And when I'd finished that little task, I popped down to the village for my appointment with Elizabeth Hampshire – the woman who'd cut short her holiday in Wales. She was also a woman who didn't bother with hot drinks, and so we had a rather unusual afternoon tea of curry puffs, lemonade and sherry.

'It's always nice to make a new friend, Georgie,' she said, patting my hand. 'I didn't manage to make your acquaintance at the ball, and I was in Davos over Christmas, which is the reason I didn't make it to your wedding, and I am sorry about that. Your aunt says it was a sensational day!'

Unsure quite what to say, I nodded, took a sip of my *Amontillado* and raised my eyebrows in an encouraging manner.

'Such a shame your husband went like he did, though, and so soon after the wedding. Still, that time in the nunnery seems to have done you good. You're positively glowing, and I hope you manage to move on as quickly as he did!'

My aunt hadn't wanted the story of my brand-new, bigamous husband's murder on our wedding night to come out – and, truth be told, neither had I.

Was His Majesty's Prison Holloway a nunnery? Of sorts, perhaps, but had my stay there done me any good? I hadn't touched a drop of champagne in seven weeks, but the preponderance of mashed potato hadn't helped my waistline one bit, although the regular self-defence episodes had certainly been invigorating. And Edward had certainly moved on; with a regimental sword buried in his chest, he'd had no choice.

When Mrs Hampshire offered me a top up of my sherry, I readily agreed and, eager to move the conversation on, I asked my aunt's friend what she knew of Bettina's missing manuscript.

'It is a mystery, isn't it?' she said, 'And something I'm very keen to get my hands on, so you really must find it! There are a lot of us counting on you.'

I reminded her that that was what I was here to do, but her story about the manuscript was as garbled as Mrs Tolliver's had been. Elizabeth said she'd been offered the manuscript to proofread after the hunt.

Given Mrs Hampshire's particularly speedy return to the Cotswolds, I had hoped she would have some valuable information to pass on, but the woman was a rabid fan, nothing more.

'I've read all of the Regency Romances and the Victoriana Vixens is a series I reread every year without fail.'

'Is that one of Lettice's?' I asked.

'Vixens? Absolutely not. Definitely one of Bettina's, although I'm sure I don't need to tell you that. You must know all of them back to front, what with your aunt being the publisher.'

I explained that I'd never so much as seen one on a bookshelf or in a shop, and after an initial gasp of surprise, she nodded enthusiastically. 'Quite right for a young woman of your age. Well, it's a kind of club, you see. One wouldn't pop into the local department store for a Michelangelo, or... into the sweet shop for a plate of Boulestin's finest, would one? One needs to be asked to partake of these treasures, they're not to everyone's taste and shouldn't be sold willy-nilly.' It took her five minutes to stop laughing at some private joke of hers, and that was only because I asked her about Mr Cullimore's passing.

'Cullimore?' she said. 'Good riddance, in my opinion. His paper was a shocker, and he was too!'

Had any of the ladies I'd questioned had a good word to say about the man? Infidelity was certainly a motive for murder, but so far, I hadn't come across mention of a single cuckolded husband. Indeed, many of my aunt's friends were unmarried. I also recalled Fiona Tolliver's words about the old man's unforgivable actions towards Anthony. What had happened there?

I realised that I'd learnt very little from all these social calls about either the murder – or the missing manuscript. Each of my aunt's friends had a different story to tell about the mysterious folder, and I was beginning to wonder whether the many trays of drinks they'd consumed at the ball, had anything to do with that.

Thirty-Five

The last on my fan club list was Freddy Basse, who I was expecting to be a woman called *Alfreda*, and I was somewhat surprised to find it was indeed a man. An old friend of my aunt's, Freddy lived in the middle of the village, just round the corner from Mrs Tolliver's home, although his interior decor was quite, quite different. While Fiona's house was a temple of good taste, Freddy's was an altar to excitement, excess and extraordinary colour. He stood at the door, wearing a close-fitting suit that would have been the thing to wear with the Beau Brummel set, but wasn't this year's cut at all. And, I noticed, as he turned, that the navy-blue suit was lined with fuchsia. Beyond the front door, there was a large papier-mâché eye with fluttering eyelashes and, unprepared for Dada in Ampney – even at this late date, I let out a short shriek.

'That's a little something I made for last year's pantomime, that they were kind enough to let me keep at the end of the run,' he explained. 'Coffee, tea, hot chocolate, cocoa or can I interest you in a really cheap and nasty glass of cooking sherry? My charwoman has drunk every drop of the decent stuff!'

It was half eleven in the morning, so I opted for a cup of tea.

'Now, how can I help you?' he asked, offering me a seat.

'I'm Georgiana – Bathsheba's niece!'

Georgie!' he yelled. 'How do you do? Gosh, it's so lovely to finally meet you. She told me you might pop round, but I had no idea it would be today. Bridge has been cancelled, so I'm all yours, for as long as you want me.'

I couldn't help laughing. 'You had no idea who I was until I sat down just now, and you invited me in anyway?'

'Kindness to strangers, my dear. The person at the front door could be a god or goddess in disguise, as you plainly are – or they could be a new friend. And besides, nobody's going to steal anything under the gaze of that eye!'

I had to agree, the eye was enormous and (apart from being made out of gluey paper) all-seeing. 'Do you do the pantomime every year? I asked.

'Freddy Bosse is the face of Ampney Amateur Dramatics. Ask anyone!' he said. 'Now, while the kettle is boiling for your dreary old tea, and before we get started, you must see my latest acquisition.'

Freddy led me into a small room off the hallway, that was mostly covered in dust sheets, but when he pulled the dull calico away, the room became a fount of glorious colours. He told me that this collection of kimono was the largest in the Western World. (In the West Country, it was almost certainly the most impressive collection, but I couldn't be sure of its status beyond Oxford.)

While he flicked through the glorious hanging silks, cottons and wools (yes, wools!), Freddy explained that there were kimono for funerals and weddings and for visiting the royal court, and kimono for aristocratic women, married women, and single women. 'I wonder which one you would wear?' he said, with a cheeky expression on his face.

'If there's a dull grey linen one, that would be about right for my current status,' I said.

'This time of year, you should be wearing *fuji-gasane*,' he said, with a flourish.

'You speak Japanese?'

'No, no, absolutely not,' said Freddy, blushing. 'I know the vocabulary necessary to describe kimono. *Fuji-gasane* means shades of wisteria, and it describes the lavender and blue colours that are traditionally worn around this time of year, or, when the cherry trees are blossoming, you can wear a cherry blossom design of course.'

'I had no idea it was so formal,' I said.

'The kimono you have in your hand, would be suitable for winter, much in the same way that we wear florals in the summer, and darker colours in the winter months.'

'I can think of one woman who'd be wearing wisteria, cherry blossom and everything floral <u>all</u> year,' I said.

'Oh, Georgie – you've met Amelia? Dear, Amelia.'

'And yet her home is so... different. I suspect her husband put his foot down.'

'Husband?' said Freddy, with a naughty glint in his eye.

'She was married, but is no longer...?' I asked, as delicately as I could.

'Well, it was a marriage of sorts, I suppose, but not in the strictest sense. Anyhow, let me see if I've got a bottle of something interesting for us to share!' When Freddy returned, he was holding small cups of *nihonshu sake* which I took gratefully, with no idea what it was. (There was no sign of the tea I'd been promised.) He told me that the drink was warm, Japanese rice wine, and it was really very pleasant. He also said that he'd told his charwoman that it was a bottle of fancy furniture polish, which was the only reason she hadn't drunk it. We sat in his courtyard garden – under the wisteria, in fact.

'Now, how was Holloway?' he asked, as we sat down; and by some miracle I didn't spill my cup of *sake* all over my lap. 'Just a guess,' he said. 'I'm right though, aren't I?'

The colour of my cheeks must have answered for me.

'Nunnery my foot!' said Freddy. 'I've been a long-time subscriber of *Domestic Bliss* and there was no question that the "G .W." who wrote all those articles about this season's must-have curtains, how to revive a floral display and the latest in flannels and towels, would run off and join a convent. You had to have gone to prison – oh and the fibs your aunt told. She has kept me entertained, I must say.'

I was most relieved that all the women I'd met hadn't been as sharp as Freddy, but it was also something of a relief to have one person to whom I wasn't playing a part. I have nothing against nuns, but it wasn't a course I was keen to pursue, although I did wonder whether that little story of my aunt's, was the reason I hadn't received a visit from the police after Mr Cullimore's demise.

Emboldened by the wine and Freddy's forthrightness, I asked my host about Dilys's cocktail fad and was told, quite strictly, NEVER to let as much as a drop of anything that woman had made touch my lips.

I told him that I'd already experienced a mouthful, and Freddy said I was lucky to be alive. 'Her concoctions are quite deadly, you know. And oh, one's head the following day…!'

'And this "marriage of sorts" you mentioned, how many of my aunt's acquaintances are we talking about?' I asked.

'Well,' said Freddy, topping up my cup, 'Fiona's a funny one. You've seen her house?'

'It's stunning!'

'Thank you,' he said, with a demure smile. 'I was given a budget and I ran with it!' Ah. So that explained the difference between Mrs Tolliver's furnishings and her fashion.

'Fiona was very generous, but you've seen Amelia's sad little home?' he asked. 'And she barely fits into that tiny little car of hers! My dear, she did not do very well at all.'

'Her house is modest, certainly, but... she didn't do well?'

'Amelia was a nurse, although I'm not sure it was the nine to five that she was being paid for,' he said, with a raised eyebrow, 'And I've heard from Fiona that she ought to have done much better than she did out of her *arrangement*.'

'What arrangement was that?' I asked.

He shrugged.

'So, are you telling me that neither of them is actually *married*?' I said, mouthing the word (and immediately wishing I hadn't).

'Chin-chin!' said Freddy, avoiding any answer.

'Chin-chin to you too.' I took a sip of my *sake*. 'But... who might Amelia have married?' I wondered out loud. 'And who might one meet, as a nurse?'

Freddy was saying nothing.

'Should she have been Amelia Ferguson?' Freddy's expression still hadn't changed, so I guessed that was wrong, and then I recalled the doctor's three children and umpteen grandchildren, and that the home that he lived in was very nice thank you – far too nice for him to be able to finance another one in the area, however small. Although, Amelia Stewart being a nurse, explained how solicitous she had been when I'd come over all funny at her house.

My *sake* finished, and covering my cup to ensure I wasn't given any more, I asked if Freddy knew anything about Bettina's missing work.

'The naughty, naughty manuscript – and in more ways than one, if Bettina's anything to do with it!' he said. 'Where could it be?'

When I suggested that it might contain names that would annoy the people involved – powerful people, Freddy stated that that was half the fun. It seemed that Freddy did, or did not, know more than he was letting on, and I wouldn't get any further this afternoon. Mr Basse was also the last person on my list of people my aunt had recommended as sources of manuscript information. I had finished my enquiries in Ampney with no better idea about its whereabouts than when I'd begun.

The manuscript was something they had or had not read. It was something they were or were not worried about. It was something they did or did not want to be featured in. It had disappeared on the day of the ball, at breakfast when they'd been waiting to read it, or in the days following. It had a blue folder not a red one. It was an absolute scream or the end of civilisation.

Thirty-Six

The day of the Art Festival, I drove my aunt to Wickbury, and we had twenty minutes before the presentation at two o'clock, to peruse the paintings.

The festival was held in churches, the town hall, family homes, a tent and the local school, so we started at St Michael & the Angels, and then crossed the road to St Saviour's before heading off to the local primary school. I'm happy to report, that the first three locations were not indicative of the higher standard of art on offer, and the churches and school were obviously housing the art they were presented with as an act of charity or education. The more serious artwork was being housed in the town hall, the home of a Mrs Grant, and the tent in which the talks were being given.

I noticed that all of the women on my aunt's list of Kiss & Swoon fans, plus Freddy of course, were present at the festival and, as I sat there, waiting for the talk to start – letting my mind wander – I realised that they had all been present in the billiard room when Francis Cullimore had been murdered. Was there any question that they were involved? I recalled the degree to which they'd all disliked the man; even Amelia Stewart had made a bit of a face when I'd mentioned him. And then I remembered that I'd had so much fun with Freddy that I hadn't thought to ask him what he thought of the dead man.

We sat down at 2pm, under billowing canvas. My aunt was there to see what she could learn about the Colours of the Cotswolds, by someone who felt a work of art that wasn't rendered in black ink, was a frippery; while I sat down to see who was in attendance.

I was pleased to see Madame Beaufort – wearing a beautiful dark green velvet, ensemble, and looking fabulous, as well as Dilys, who looked a lot more relaxed than most people would be at the first event of a festival they'd arranged. I wondered if she'd enjoyed a glass or two of Ampney Rocket before she'd arrived – and then I saw him!

Leo Adlington was lurking at the back of the hall, lighting a cigarette with the stub of his last, and looking furtive. He appeared to be on the look-out for someone he wanted to avoid and, when the tent flap opened and a dozen new people arrived, he bobbed down, seemingly unaware that half the female eyes in the room were glancing his way. Despite his ludicrous behaviour and chain-smoking, he was much the most attractive man in the room. Leo's olive skin, dark curls and intense eyebrows were a definite plus in a tent mostly populated by women – and the few men present were... well, a lot less Byronic, let's say.

'He's picturesque,' said my aunt, 'I'll give you that, but I don't fancy your chances against Mrs Andrews, Ruby Parr or the vicar's wife. Those pews don't move themselves. She has a formidable arm.'

'I don't know what you're talking about,' I said, and I *almost* added that, thanks to my time inside, I was well able to hold my own (but Lady Fortune looked kindly on me, and she held my tongue).

The tent flapped open again, and another five people entered – Thomas Bower and Peter Cullimore among them. And when I looked towards the back of the tent again, there was no sign of Adlington – crouched, or otherwise.

If I could have made it out of the tent to follow him, I would have, but my aunt and I were boxed in, and subjected to an hour's impassioned speech by an artist who drew, printed and painted using only Indian ink.

The techniques of hatching, cross-hatching, scribbling, stippling and smudging were described in quite some detail, and the argument for working only in black and white was made with some force, but evidently not enough to keep my Aunt Bathsheba awake. I gave her a nudge and she awoke with a violent start, yelling, 'Gilgamesh!' at the top of her voice. Surprisingly, she wasn't the only woman in the tent to have yelled something similar, and I was only grateful that it had been the name of one of her cats, and not the name of someone else's husband. (Unless the curate's wife has a cat called Reginald, she's going to have some questions to answer, that's all I'll say.)

By the time Mr Tingle's talk drew to a close, the outer ring of chairs was empty, and the only people remaining were those who, like me, had been boxed in by sleepers. Shuffling his papers, Tingle asked if anyone had any questions and, when one woman put her hand up, the glares she received were sufficient that she told the lecturer that she would speak to him afterwards.

And so, we trooped out of that tent, and into another. A tent full of scones, clotted cream, strawberry jam, and gallons and gallons of tea. Bliss.

'Well, I never thought that would end,' said my aunt.

'No, neither did I,' drinking half a cup of tea in one long sip. I was still anxious to see Mr Adlington, but more anxious to revive myself after the last hour and a half. 'What I don't understand,' I said, 'Is why someone would give a lecture on something like that. Colour is fine, monochrome is fine. It's merely a question of artistry and ability. I mean, who would argue that watercolour was a more pleasing medium than oils?'

'Or, indeed, sculpture,' said my aunt, her gaze evidently caught by something. Or someone.

I looked over and saw Adlington – closely followed by Peter Cullimore, and the two of them were having a heated discussion, that was, unfortunately for me, being hissed and whispered, rather than bellowed. I didn't catch a word they said, but the emotions behind it were plain to see. Anger and lots of prodding from Peter, anger, annoyance and being prodded from Adlington.

Leo was waiting for his drink, when Peter had obviously said something that was a step too far; he turned and shoved Peter into the table, and strode out as teapots, cups and saucers clattered to the floor. I ran over to see if I could help – well, sort of help. 'Peter! What was that about?'

'A little misunderstanding,' he said.

'An artistic misunderstanding?'

'Not entirely,' said the man, brushing scone crumbs from his trousers. 'A problem with a... with a model.'

'Anyone I know?'

He didn't say anything, but got up, smiled and thanked the lady hiding behind the kettle, who had managed to save him a single cup and saucer and was offering him tea, and he stalked out of the tent without another word. I wasn't going to let my own tea and scones go to waste by following him, so I returned to my table.

'What was that about?' asked my aunt.

‘It seems they’ve got model problems,’ I said. ‘One model, two artists.’ They could have been “sharing” any number of models, but I suspected it was Loretta that had been the cause of that little ding-dong, and I wondered which of them was paying her nursing home bills – and expecting to whisk her away any day soon.

‘Sharing a model is always a tricky proposition,’ said my aunt. ‘I recall, when I was much younger, having two artists fighting over me – unfortunately, the wrong one won, and my dear! The portrait at the end of it. Well, it’s in the attic, and not getting any older, either. And the other one – who couldn’t string enough of a sentence together to win me over – he went on to gain a place at the Royal Academy. Such a shame.’

‘But being a member of the Royal Academy is a fine thing, isn’t it?’

She patted my hand. ‘A shame for me, my dear. I could have been hanging on the wall of their hallowed halls.’

Thirty-Seven

The tent was full of the great, the good, the mediocre, the nosy and the seriously well-off of our area, all of them examining the art on display through spectacles, pince-nez and screwed-up eyes. I passed three local vicars, a couple of well-to-do farmers and half of my aunt's bridge club. Dr Ferguson was also in attendance, which was just as well, as the average age at the function was high and, in addition to the gallons of tea and mountains of cake on offer, there was scrumpy for sale. I don't touch the stuff; even regular cider is too much for me, but this local brew was lethal, and being sold in jam jars.

'Ferguson!' said my aunt, 'Has anything caught your eye?'

'I'm not much for this artistic stuff, but there's a still life in the corner that I could find a home for. Have you found anything interesting?'

'These local shindigs are tricky,' said my aunt, 'When one has a Holbein and a Constable hanging at home, it is difficult to sully the walls, however well-intentioned the artists are.'

(The Holbein was nothing of the sort, and the Constable she had was not the type you're thinking of. In both cases, the frames were worth more than the paintings, but I bit my lip.)

They turned to other, less contentious matters – or maybe not. 'It looks like your garden's safe, Mrs Godfrey.'

'Really? That's jolly good news.'

'It seems there was a bit of a mix-up in the laboratory.'

'Yes,' I said. 'We heard about that. And?'

'And Old Cullimore's passing is recorded as death by an overdose of one of his regular medications.'

'So, there was nothing nefarious about it, after all?' asked my aunt.

'No, just one of those things,' he said.

I was tempted to say, 'One of those murderous things?' but the man looked so relieved. There was no question at all that somebody had tried to run me off the road. Loretta was frightened and hiding – and someone had done their best to prevent her from seeing to her employer at the ball, as he lay dying. If anger was a symptom of grief, then so be it, but it could also be a symptom of guilt – and the man's grandson, Anthony, had anger to spare.

There was more to Old Cullimore's death than a slip of the hand.

While my aunt haggled with the curator over a canvas of a horse; "It's very large and it would be just the thing to cover a crack in a wall that is letting in the most dreadful draught!" I left the tent in search of the artists. One of them had to be the key to the Loretta mystery, at least.

Twenty minutes later, I had found neither, and I'd had enough of the festival. I'd eaten scones, I'd listened to a man blather on about ink for far too long, and I'd looked at bad, middling and some quite good art and I could afford none of it, besides which, I had nowhere to hang the stuff.

'Dilys is driving me back,' said my aunt. 'We're off to the next gallery along to see the results of a life drawing class – and I told her you wouldn't be interested, and you look like you've had enough. Why don't you go home?'

'Still life, did you say?'

'A still life with people in it, yes. Off home with you!'

Relieved not to have to wait around, I was going to drive home, but the Sunbeam had different ideas. I lifted the bonnet, but had no idea what I was looking at, so I lowered it again. I tried the key in the ignition, but still nothing more than a weak moan from the engine. I lowered my forehead to the wheel – a gesture of disappointment – and the bruise on my temple immediately reminded me of why this beautiful car might not be at its best. Perhaps the bloke in the pick-up truck's assessment hadn't been accurate. He'd dragged it out of the mud and when it had started, he'd asked for his money and disappeared. And then I heard a voice. I looked up to see Leo Adlington. His shirt was slightly torn from his encounter with Peter Cullimore, earlier in the day, and he looked quite perfect.

'In need of a hand?' he asked.

'That would be wonderful. I don't suppose you know how these things work?' I asked.

'I was hoping you were going to ask me to give you a push, or wind the handle at the front,' he said. 'I don't even drive, let alone know how to fix one of them.'

He misinterpreted my smile of relief, as judgment of some kind, and he stalked off muttering something about never finding the time, and 'it can't be as tricky as it looks'. If Leo Adlington couldn't drive, there was no way he could have driven me off the road, on the way back from the Breakwater Cottage

Hospital, although he could still be the father of Loretta's baby, of course.

And while I was pondering that, Freddy joined me.

'Enjoying the festival?' he asked.

'Wonderful!' I said.

'It is very kind of you to say so,' he said, 'And you'll be coming tomorrow?'. His cocksure confidence during my visit with him earlier in the week was gone. The festival was Dilys and Freddy's lovechild, and if I'd even so much as hinted that the hours spent listening to the intricacies of shading in ink hadn't been my cup of tea, I think our friendship would have soured instantly.

'Tomorrow is a talk on watercolours, isn't it?' I asked, congratulating myself that I'd done so well to remember.

'That's in the afternoon,' he said, 'You'll have to arrive a little earlier for the talk on macramé – which Dilys is doing herself,' he said. I thought I saw a hint of embarrassment, and was relieved when he said, 'The watercolour might be more your thing. Be sure to tell Bettina about the macrame when you see her. Playing with knots is one of her strengths.' And the Freddy I knew, was back.

'I don't suppose you know anything about engines,' I said, tapping the bonnet, and not thinking for a moment he wou ld.Ten minutes later, my Sunbeam was right as rain. It seemed that Freddy knew quite a lot about cars. 'What do you drive?' I asked.

'At the moment, that monster over there,' he said, pointing at a dark blue car, the sight of which rang a bell. And the scrapes on the paintwork made that bell ring even louder.

I thanked Freddy for his help with the car, and stumbled away, babbling something about having to see a nude.

Thirty-Eight

It seemed impossible that Fred Basse, who had shown me the highlights of his kimono collection and introduced me to the delights of *sake*, could have been behind the wheel of a vehicle that had almost run me off the road. He was also someone who had guessed what had become of me during my time away, and hadn't reckoned me the nun that my aunt had said I was. A formidable adversary indeed, I staggered back into the tent, and into the strong capable arms – of an art dealer.

'Oh, Mr Bowers!' I said.

'Georgie! Please – call me Tom.' He seemed a little surprised that I'd rushed into his arms in the way that I had, so I made some excuse about tripping over a guy rope, and extricated myself from his embrace.

'So, how are you enjoying the festival?' he asked.

'Very good. And avoiding the dead fish on pewter, as per your instructions.'

'Yes, yes...' he said, but he couldn't quite raise a smile.

'So, you're back in the Cotswolds?' I said, trying to look as if I was paying him the requisite amount of attention, but cocking an eye in the direction of the tent flap, to see if Freddy would follow me in. It was unlikely he would mow me down a second time, in the middle of a tent surrounded by so many onlookers and potential victims, but I couldn't be sure. Every time I heard a car pass, I couldn't help stiffening a little.

'Well, the bottom fell out of the market, and the bank manager has insisted that I change course. It's all very well following one's dream, one's artistic *raison d'être*, but one has to eat. And so, dead fish on pewter plates it is.'

'I'm sorry, dead what?'

'Fish,' he said. 'On pewter plates. Still lives.'

'Oh, right,' I said, and I caught my breath as I spotted Freddy over the other side of the tent and he gave me a brief wave and a cheery, but slightly concerned smile. He may have been the face of Ampney Amateur Dramatics, but if he was the killer, there was nothing amateur about his acting. He evidently didn't know that I'd guessed that his was the car that had driven my beloved Sunbeam into a ditch, so I remained safe. For the moment.

My heart was still racing and, when Tom asked me if I fancied a drink, I readily agreed. After a long sip of mead (it wasn't what I'd asked for, but it was the only thing left), I said to him, 'I hope this won't sound rude, but Wickbury isn't Mayfair. They may have an art festival, but it's hardly Bruton Street.'

'No, no, indeed,' he said, 'But I grew up in this village.'

'Ah, yes, I did hear someone mention something like that... Do you still have family in the area?'

'Not in Wickbury,' he said, 'But my sister Amelia is in the next one along.'

'Mrs Stewart? We've met. I'm sure I saw her earlier, at the back of the tent.'

'Art really isn't her thing at all, she's a much more practical woman, but happy to show a bit of familial support.'

I thought back to Mrs Stewart's modest little home, but her walls were bare.

'Her purchases kept me going for a while, I can tell you. A very nice little nest egg she had there.'

'And presumably a sister gets a discount?' I asked, with what I hoped was a cheeky smile.

'She would,' he said, 'But of course it was, well, it was her – her husband who bought them.'

'Of course,' I said. 'Amelia's husband.'

And as Thomas nodded, he gave the almost imperceptible twitch of the eyes that told me he was playing along. Freddy had suggested as much; "Mr Stewart", whoever he was, had bankrolled Amelia's art. And, judging by the current state of her walls, her brother had sold it on when times had got tough. I suspected there was more to be found out about this woman – all of the fans on my aunt's list in fact, and the police might think the Cullimore case was resolved, but I didn't.

Thirty-Nine

After the problem I'd had with the Sunbeam at the festival which, admittedly, Freddy Basse had fixed, I wanted to have the car checked out. Baxter told me that his son, Bert, would give me a good rate, and so it was, that I drove the sunbeam onto the cobbles of the local garage forecourt.

The chief mechanic introduced himself to me, and I vaguely recalled having seen him on the estate before the war – when he'd been my uncle's driver, and Baxter, his father, had worked as a handyman around the house. Now, of course, Bert's father was the handyman AND the chauffeur, and ten years older than he'd been when my uncle had brought him out of semi-retirement.

The Younger Baxter consulted a large red ledger to see when they might be able to fit me in, despite the fact that his two young apprentices had been playing cards when I'd arrived, and there wasn't a raised car bonnet to be seen.

When he suggested 'A week, Tuesday?' I gave him the Auntie Bathsheba eyebrow, crossed my arms, pursed my lips and suggested they might have time now? He flicked the page back, took the pencil from behind his ear and asked me my name.

Bert entered me into the book – and the clock struck one. Both his junior mechanics were given leave to have their lunch, and they skipped out of the garage like a couple of puppies.

'I can see she's been in the wars,' he said.

'Which was nothing to do with my driving,' I assured him, as I stroked her bonnet. 'I'd also like you to give her a tune-up and an oil change. She hasn't been starting as she should.'

The mechanic told me he would get straight to it. I asked him when I should return, and he said to come back in a couple of hours' time, and if he hadn't fixed it by then, he'd have a better idea of how long it would take. And that was when I spotted Freddy's car. His magnificent beast – the car I'd seen him with at the Art Festival. The machine that almost ended my life.

'This car belongs to Freddy Basse, doesn't it?' I said, bending down to examine its bumper for flecks of the Sunbeam's oxblood-red paint.

'The Duchess?' he said. 'No. His Riley spent a couple of days with us, but it's running very nicely now. He picked it up this morning.'

'So, this isn't his?'

'No,' he said, giving it an affectionate pat, 'This grand old lady is what we lend to our long-term customers, if theirs are out of action and they need a set of wheels for a day or two. Some of them won't take her. Say she's too big, too much to handle, but Mr Basse has driven her a few times.'

I had to get hold of that ledger, and find out who had been running around with the Duchess the afternoon I visited Loretta at the nursing home.

I walked over to the Sunbeam and tugged at a cable. There was a spurt of oil and I called Bert over. (I'm not proud of myself for doing that, but something had to be done.)

'I think there's something wrong!' I called out. 'You see here, there's a bit of a mess...'

'What on earth has happened here?' While Bert bent down to examine the source of the oil, I asked if I might use his telephone and, distracted by my spot of chaos, he nodded and began to apply himself to working out how the cable could have come loose. While he was busy, I lifted the receiver and made the odd talky-talky noise, while scanning the big, red book.

I looked at the previous Thursday and, peering at bad handwriting amid oily finger prints and tea stains, I deduced that three people had had their cars in the garage that day. One was a lady by the name of 'Ethel R.' whose car was in for an hour – and it just said *"clean + fill w/ petrol"* next to it. Not the most demanding job they'd ever received.

The second entry was for "*Cullimore*", but Anthony or Peter? I noticed an instruction written next to it, "Drop at Kemble. Ready for pick up Friday at 4.15pm." Whichever of the two men it was, had been dropped off at the station, and returned the following day on the train. Neither of the Cullimores had been driving the deadly Duchess.

And the third name? *"A. Stuart".* Assuming they'd got the spelling wrong, that was another name I recognised.

I quickly flicked the book back to today's page, and realised I still had the telephone receiver in my hand. Saying a loud, 'Cheerio!' I plonked it down as the mechanic stood upright – and noticed the state of his dungarees. My beautiful Sunbeam had suffered for my investigation, and I hoped it would understand.

'Well, that was odd,' he said. 'The cable didn't look loose when I popped my head under the bonnet two minutes ago.

Still, these things happen. We'll give her the once over, Mrs Mortimer, cables included. Shouldn't take too long.'

'That's excellent news,' I said, fishing a coin out of my purse. 'And thank you for allowing me to use your telephone. Here – to cover the cost of the call,' I said, laying it on the table. A penny for that little nugget of information about the Duchess, was cheap at half the price, but it was best to check, so I told him, 'Baxter recommended your place of course, but I was also told about you by Amelia. She was very impressed.'

He looked a little confused. Had I got the wrong woman?

'Amelia, Amelia... I don't think I know an -'

'Amelia Stewart,' I said.

'Oh! You mean Matron!' he said. 'Yes, yes, we've been seeing her for years. Once a car is fixed by us it is fixed, it's just that her Austin doesn't tend to stay fixed. Trouble with everything.'

'It's in here a lot?'

'A fair bit,' he admitted, 'But my dad was in her class at school, so I give her a good price.'

'And she borrows the Duchess when her car is in the garage?'

'She does. It's twice the size of her Austin, but she's happy to take it. We've told her it would be cheaper to get a new car, but she won't think of it. Says while it can be fixed, she wants it fixed. It's costing her an arm and a leg, though.' The mechanic went on, at pains to make it clear that their garage wouldn't just string someone along and keep on repairing something that couldn't be saved. When he told me that I would catch up with her if I picked my car up later – she was coming in to drop hers off at four. I thanked him for his information, and said that I'd be back long before then.

I wandered round the corner to the Rose Tea Gardens, and over a pot of tea and poached eggs on toast, I pondered Mrs

Stewart's sentimentality about a car that was costing her a small fortune, when she was a woman who had managed to make it to the rank of "matron", and had presumably had access to any number of drugs during her working life. I also recalled that when I'd paid her a visit, I'd told her that my next appointment was at a hospital.

And when I'd finished the pondering and the poached eggs – and ordered a second pot, I began to wonder why Amelia Stewart had followed me to the nursing home, and then tried to kill me.

Forty

The following morning, the sky was the colour of lead; flat and grey, and pelting with rain.

I lay on my bed, unsure what to do next – aside from eating the honeyed-toast and tea the maid had just brought me. I had to find out why Amelia Stewart had tried to run me off the road – that would require some delicate handling. I also wanted to know who the father of Loretta's child was, which would require even more delicate handling.

And I also had questions about Anthony Cullimore's relationship with his grandfather. What was the unforgivable thing that Old Cullimore had done to his grandson, that Fiona Tolliver had mentioned? Where was the will that Fiona's brother, Cullimore's solicitor, had waylaid? And where, oh where was Bettina's manuscript?

With too much to think about, I listened to the sounds outside, and there was something about the dull light and the pitter-patter that reminded me of Holloway. Constant footsteps and the grey everything – the clothes, the walls, the food. I was so glad to be out, but I still felt a pang of pity for my friends inside, and guilt that I was free and they weren't. There was only one thing to be done; a visit to the sweet shop.

I called Crumpet, who needed to get out of the house, even if she wasn't strictly speaking being taken for a walk, and I pulled on my mac. We jumped in the Sunbeam and drove to the centre of town, which was awash, and understandably quiet. Shop doors were shut and waiting for a suitable time to declare themselves closed. I parked as close as I could to the sweetshop just off the high street and, when the vicious gust whipping at my wheels died down, I took my chances and opened the car door. Crumpet encouraged me with weak barks; keen to stay in the car, on her blanket. I fairly jumped the six feet from the car door to the step, and plunged inside the sweetshop, dripping all over the floor and, as the bell sounded, little Mrs Kibby popped up, behind the counter.

According to my Uncle Lawrence, she had been in attendance since his father was a boy, which didn't seem possible, but if she really was that old – and looked as good as she did – it certainly suggested that sixpence of chocolate limes was as good a use of my meagre resources as any amount of cold cream. (And, before you ask, no, I didn't tell the old lady that I was buying for my prison chums.)

There were jars of clove rocks, brandy balls and wine gums. There were bags of peanut brittle, liquorice allsorts and jelly babies, tins of Parma violets and aniseed balls, blocks of toffee and fudge, and boxes of chocolates and candied fruits, and more besides. In short, there was everything I could think of.

I bought fourpence each of mint humbugs, chocolate limes, barley sugars and lemon sherbets, knowing that the wrapped sweets were better suited to yard time swapsies. I bought a bar of marzipan for Auntie Bathsheba, a bar of nougat for Uncle Lawrence, a bag of pear drops to share with Maude, and a single aniseed ball, to see if little dogs really are as fond of them as people like to suggest they are.

And as I was settling up, I wondered just how old Mrs Kibby might be and it crossed my mind that she must have come across Old Cullimore more than most, so I asked her about him.

'Who?'

'Francis Cullimore.'

'No. You're still mumbling,' she said.

'FRANCIS CULLIMORE,' I yelled. 'OLD CULLIMORE!'

'Nothing old about him!' said Mrs K, and for a moment, I was afraid she was going to put the sweets back. 'He ran the paper. Had a son who died, and looked after his son's little one in turn.'

'Yes – Anthony!'

'Used to bring him in for a bag of liquorice bullets the first Saturday of every month,' she said.

'Sweets once a month?' I said, 'Well, I suppose it was better for his teeth than having them regularl-'

'THAT is a mistake a lot of people make,' she said. 'I think you'll find that sugar *cleans* your teeth.'

'Of course,' I said, sucking on a pear drop, and vainly hoping she was right.

'And the boy did get his sweets every Saturday, because those other weeks he was brought in by his nurse. She was very kind to him. Almost like a second mother.'

'That's good to know,' I said with a smile and I meant it. Losing one's parents so young, must have been a terrible shock for him. He had been very young of course, but with a sickly grandmother and only his rather gruff grandfather to look after him, it was just as well he'd had a well-meaning nurse while he was growing up.

I thanked Mrs Kibby for the armful of confectionery, and opened the door. The rain hadn't abated and, after a bit of a struggle with Crumpet and that aniseed ball, I put the remaining goodies into the glove compartment, and I was about to drive off, when I noticed someone coming out of the office next door. There was something familiar about her, as she struggled to open the umbrella, shut the door behind her, and keep the file she held, under her arm. I noticed a sign swinging above her head, and realised it was the office of Tolliver & Co., the local solicitor. The woman wrestling with the floral umbrella was his sister Fiona – and the file under her arm, was Bettina's manuscript!

When she'd got her umbrella unfurled and the door shut, Fiona Tolliver looked back and forth before stepping out from the front of the Sunbeam, to cross the road, and I hoped she hadn't seen me. The rain was hard enough that it was unlikely, but I was only ten feet away, and I slunk down in my seat until I was sure she had crossed. What was she doing with Bettina's manuscript?

I took a deep breath, and then drove thirty minutes away, to a post office in Inglesham where there was less chance of my being recognised.

I mixed the bags of wrapped sweets together, divided them into three, and posted them to my roommate, Ivy, my lock-pick tutor, Marjorie, and Phyllida the suffragist and self-defence specialist. All of them residents of G Wing, Holloway Prison, London N7.

If the postmistress was surprised that I was sending parcels to prisoners, she was good enough not to say anything, and I returned to Ampney. A trip to the library was in order.

Forty-One

I recalled my last trip to see the librarian, Mrs Burrows, sitting in her tiny little office while she examined her calendar, and of seeing the ring-bound spines of similar calendars, covering an entire wall. The whole thing had looked faintly woolly at the time, but there was nothing woolly about the information they held. She had a record of the entire village's comings and goings, and if she and Mr Tolliver ever got together, they'd have the private lives, financial dealings and the comings and goings of the entire area's residents all sewn up. I wondered if Military Intelligence knew what Mrs Burrows got up to, and whether they had ever tried to recruit her.

It was almost closing time when I arrived, the rain was still relentless, but the library was full of people – and also full of volunteers. The local girls' school encouraged their pupils to help out when they could, and so Mrs Burrows was at a loose end, and obviously desperate to speak with someone over the age of fifteen.

I was curious to know who Mr Cullimore's previous nurses had been, and I asked her if she could find that out for me. I knew she wouldn't give me the information straight off the bat, and that a little *quid pro quo* was called for, so I told her that the police had dropped the investigation into the murder of Old Mr Cullimore which, of course, she knew. What else did I know that might be of interest to her... I was going to have to either make something up or drop someone in it. Who, who, who?

Leo's nude sketches of locals? No, that was a step too far. And then I looked up and saw the daubs of Peter Cullimore that lined the library walls. I spoke with her about his artistic bent, and wondered idly what his father made of it. It wasn't exactly a nugget of gossip, but it got her chatting on a subject we were both able to engage in; the odd relationship between Anthony and son, which led to a conversation about Anthony and his grandfather, which eventually led us round to the old man's many nurses.

'I wondered if you might be able to tell me who Mr Cullimore's former nurses have been?' I asked. 'Only his will is missing, and I thought one of them might be able to help me find it.'

'His will is missing?' she said. Her eyes were open wide, and I imagined little cogs beginning to whirr – working out who she could tell that little gem to, and what she might get back. (I had, of course, assumed she knew about the will, otherwise I would have begun with that, and not wasted the last five minutes.)

Mrs Burrows readily agreed to help me and scuttled into her tiny little office, with me in tow. Rifling through the rows of calendars, she plucked out all the ones with a stripe of red at the bottom – the ones that were *labelled "Nurses & Companions"*, and she must have gathered up forty years' worth of information. And she was about to open one of them up, when something crossed her mind. 'I'm not en-ti-re-ly sure that I should be showing you this.' Her eyes had narrowed, but I got the comforting feeling that, rather than evaluating *my* motives, she was trying to find some way around this legal bump in the road. 'Hm.' She sank down to her seat, and I sank with her. 'Well, while I give it some thought, let me just get the ones that I think might be of most use.'

'Would the fact that he's dead help?' I asked. (I wasn't sure how that question came across as I said it, but she seemed to take it in the right spirit.)

'Perhaps... now, if I recall correctly, he began employing nurses when he turned sixty or so, so that would be about 1885 onwards, although of course, at that point they weren't actually for him. They were for his wife, who was becoming weaker by the day. Before her death, Mrs Cullimore insisted on the nurses being married ladies, but after she went to her eternal rest – and when Mr Cullimore needed a new carer, that was no longer a concern. And he had quite a string of them.'

'Interesting that he didn't keep that little rule going,' I said.

'I thought so,' agreed Mrs Burrows, 'Although to be fair, the original advert we agreed on stipulated "married, with nursing experience", but we were never asked to check, which is just as well really, because a great many women had to find work. And if you were a certain age and unmarried, people could be funny about it, however much experience you had. and besides, if you can't trust someone to be married and decent when they've got the ring on, then you can't trust them to look after you at delicate moments, can you?'

'Absolutely,' I said in agreement, hoping I'd understood what she meant, and marvelling that, when it came to really practical jobs, the necessary marital status was the opposite of that required at an office. Either way, I couldn't help sympathising with the many women who'd had to change their status in order to survive, myself included.

'As you say, Old Mr Cullimore has been gathered to God,' she went on, 'So it would be in the spirit of investigation, rather than nosiness, if you were to see those names. As you say, the young or not-so-young women might know where he kept his paperwork and that's really a legal matter, isn't it.'

'A matter of civic duty,' I agreed, nodding.

'Hm,' she said, and she put her hand to her ear – hearing a non-existent call for her assistance. 'Sounds like somebody needs me... I shall be back in five minutes.'

The initials on the front page were the clients, and the ones on the back page were those of the nurses and companions. If I was right, then Francis William Cullimore was the FWC who had a nurse from twelve to 6pm every day of the week except Tuesday, as well as the odd special occasion – like my aunt's ball. The nurse for 1926 till now was listed as LS; Loretta using her stage name for her nursing initials – which made a sort of sense, seeing as she was, to all intents and purposes playing a part there too.

Prior to that, there were decades of a selection of women, none of them long-lived – from an employment point of view. Certainly, no names sprang to my attention, and the names began a lot later than I'd been led to believe. Who had worked for his wife, Dora? There was nobody listed under the initials, "D.C.".

I left the library and hurried back to the estate. It had been a long day, and the sooner I got Crumpet back home, the better. I had learned more about Mrs Burrows ethics, than I had about old Mr Cullimore's.

Forty-Two

My aunt was playing cards with her cronies, Uncle Lawrence was poring over some work he had to do, Crumpet was spending the evening being tutored by Maude, and the writers had gone out to a dance. They had invited me along to their shindig in Stow-On-the-Wold, but when they asked, I'd only just got in from the library, and my feet were still wet. I was now dry and warm, my teeth were jangling from too many boiled sweets, and I was feeling restless.

The clock struck nine and I realised that it was already 'lights out' for the Holloway inmates. A month ago, I would have been settling down to tell Ivy a story. Or she would have been telling me something equally diverting about one of her eleven siblings.

There were a lot of things I did not miss about being inside, but what I did miss at the moment was camaraderie – and certainty, although, rethinking that, I realised that while I was in prison, I hadn't known what was going to happen from one day to the next. I had spent my time inside, awaiting the court case that loomed ahead of me, and there had been no certainty about the outcome of that.

Nostalgia is a dreadful thing, and being nostalgic for prison was a step beyond, but one very good thing had come out of my 'time with the ladies' as my aunt referred to it, and that was my ability to pick a lock.

I wondered how long my aunt would be at her bridge club, and went in search of Maude, who was in the ballroom, trying to teach Crumpet how to roll over and beg. She told me that Bathsheba would be back at about midnight – and that she would stay later, if it weren't for Baxter. 'The standard of his driving dips terribly if he's tired. Hopefully he'll have had a kip in the car while she's playing, and she'll stay longer if she's winning, of course. Might bow out early, if she isn't – AND BEG! GOOD GIRL!'

I thanked Maude for her information, patted clever little Crumpet and went upstairs to the wardrobe full of Louisa's clothes, that I'd been dipping into for the last couple of weeks. After a little root around, I found a pair of black silk pyjamas which, teamed with Jack's beret and my uncle's scarf, made for a fairly good outfit for *ferreting-around-at-night*. I also stumbled across a pair of black plimsolls that belonged to my aunt, although what she was doing with them, I couldn't imagine.

By the time I sneaked out to the Sunbeam with a handful of hairgrips and a hat pin that my uncle had stepped on and bent out of shape – out of shape for a hat, but just right for a lock-pick. My blood was up, and I was feeling pretty pleased with myself, until I heard Crumpet barking, and the front door was opened by my uncle, with Maude leaning over his shoulder, with Crumpet under her arm.

I'm just off to... meet a friend,' I called out – with the key already in the ignition.

'Very good,' said my uncle.

'Are you going to take the dog for a walk?' yelled Maude, striding over to the car. It had just begun to spit with rain, and it became clear that she was made of sterner stuff than the dog was. Little Crumpet began to whine, but was firmly placed her in the seat beside me.

I was surprised neither of them asked me more about what I intended to do dressed head to toe in black, at this time of night, and then I remembered that I'm a 28-year-old woman and allowed to do whatever I want. Well... within the law, anyway.

I gave Lawrence and Maude a last little wave, and may have accidentally allowed Crumpet's lead to slip from my fingers and, as the two of them retreated into the hallway, the little dog jumped out of the car window, sprang up the steps and slithered through the door like a shot of quicksilver, back into the warm.

A small, talkative dog wasn't helpful on this occasion: I was off to retrieve the missing manuscript that I'd seen under Fiona Tolliver's arm, and I could only imagine the look on my aunt's face when I returned it to her!

I drove the Sunbeam into Ampney and, needless to say, parking was not a problem at this time of night. I adjusted my beret and looked down at the outfit I was wearing. Satin pyjamas, even black ones, tend to shine, and I hoped that wasn't going to be a problem, but I couldn't help feeling I should have opted for the dark green tweed skirt and jacket instead.

Just around the corner from Fiona's home, I looked up and down the street and, aside from a man walking his dog, there was nobody about, so I bent down and pretended to adjust my shoe or my handbag or something. Man and dog passed: the coast was clear and the rain had subsided. I opened Mrs Tolliver's gate –

or rather, I began to open her gate, and I immediately recalled the terrible squeaking sound it had made days before. I stopped pushing, and realised that I hadn't brought my pot of Vaseline with me. I also realised that the gap I'd opened was nowhere near wide enough for my hips.

I was going to have to scrabble over the wall. Fortunately, plimsolls are just the thing – although the knees of the pyjamas would never be the same again. I jumped over the other side and tried not to make too much noise when I made contact with a holly bush, and stepped from that, into a rose bush with horns like a rhinoceros. When I had stopped stifling my bellows – a beret stuffed in the mouth is remarkably good for this – I assessed Fiona's property. There were no lights on, and the coast looked clear. I ran from one shadow to the next, across the grass, and made it to her door. Still no one there, so I knocked on the door; which I hadn't meant to do.

My mind raced with how I'd explain my presence at this time of night, and I realised that the excitement of being attacked by her foliage may have clouded my mind. I took a deep breath, and a step back, and was relieved that no one actually answered – at which point I congratulated myself on ensuring that the mistress was not at home.

Taking another deep breath, I got the hatpin and hairgrips out of my pocket, and felt their ends in the darkness, establishing which tool was which. And then I began to work at her lock. A front door is a tricky thing, and requires a lot more precision and patience than a cabinet lock.

I slid in the tension lever (the hatpin) and turned the cylinder and then, keeping the pressure on, I slid in the "fiddling stick" (Marjorie's name for it, not mine), and I began to listen for the click each time, easing it in and up until the pins lifted halfway, and with each click, the hatpin was pushed a little further, until I felt the door open. I allowed myself a moment to relax – holding my hands firm, and remembering to breathe. The door opened much more quietly than the gate had done, and I slipped inside – as a grey-coloured cat slipped out. Bother!

Forty-Three

I crept across the hallway to the kitchen, where I found the cat's plate of fish – I wouldn't be able to concentrate while that cat was roaming about. Tapping the plate with a spoon, I miaowed as loudly as I hoped a cat would, and within two minutes the cat – a Siamese – had returned. It was a miracle! The little animal lapped up the fish, licked its chops and slunk back into the night, out of the door I hadn't closed properly. Bother again!

Time was of the essence, so for the time being, I would have to forget about the escapee. The study was smart and very tidy, and I wished I'd had the foresight to have a proper look around when I'd had the chance; a pocket torch is all very well, but not as good as broad daylight. None of the drawers in the bureau in the corner were locked – and none of them contained the manuscript. The bookshelves were similarly manuscript-free.

I moved on to her sitting room, which was every bit as elegant as I remembered, except that the floorboards squeaked, which was something I didn't recall from my visit a week ago. After a little experimentation, I realised, I was safest walking around the room's edges. The coal scuttle held no secrets, the fireplace was still warm, and not likely to be hiding anything made of paper, and the expansive armchairs were innocent enough.

I moved onto the bathroom, which was chic, refined and minimalist in its lines – until I opened the bathroom cabinet, which was crammed full of everything under the sun, including a tube of denture cream, which was understandable for a woman of her age, except that her teeth looked sufficiently tea-stained and wonky to be the genuine article. If the denture cream was hers, I wondered who made her false teeth. It was a bizarre vanity.

As I closed the cabinet door, I realised that one thing this cabinet did not contain, was anything medicinal of any kind. No tinctures, powders or salves. Where did the solicitor's sister keep her aspirin? I put everything back where I'd found it, and moved on to the bedroom, which was awash with flower prints, and everything that her elegant sitting room was not, but still no sign of a manuscript.

My tour of the kitchen revealed that the biscuit jar contained shortbread, the tea caddy contained the dreaded chamomile, and the bread bin contained half a Chelsea bun.

I opened up everything I could find, including the cupboard under the sink, which housed a veritable pharmacy. There was aspirin, pepto-bismol, soda-mints, plasters, calamine lotion, a jar of Virol, castor oil, rat poison, cod liver oil, and an impressive selection of bandages and plasters. I supposed that, if one's cooking weren't up to scratch, one might need the medication a little closer to hand than the bathroom, but still... no sign of a file.

One more room to search – which must be the dining room, or similar. I closed the kitchen cabinet, and was about to cross the hallway, when I heard footsteps and the sound of a key in the door. Had I locked it after the cat had come in? I slid behind the coat stand and shrank back as the key turned and, as the door opened, Fiona stepped in – followed by the cat which, by her reaction, she hadn't realised had just stepped inside with her. Thank goodness, well, apart from the fact that I was trapped in the woman's home, and I had not been invited.

I heard Mrs Tolliver walking about, and the familiar sound of a woman easing off uncomfortable shoes. The cat was good enough to run up and greet her – and not then run over to me and dob me in. I stayed where I was, stock still, and the lady of the house left the study and was standing within a hair's breadth of me; but she'd been good enough not to turn the lights on, and I remained hidden behind green velvet. I heard the familiar tinkle of a teaspoon in a glass, the sound of Fiona mixing herself a bedtime drink, and of her retiring to her sitting room and turning the wireless on. It was the shipping forecast.

While the announcer warned of *"Gales in Cromarty, Forties, Forth and Tyne"*, I squeezed out of my hiding place, and while he reported *"Showers and westerlies in Fastnet, Lundy and North Fitzroy"*, I tried the front door and realised my luck had run out. She had locked it, of course, and I didn't think I had time to pick it before the forecast finished and I was found out.

And so, I found myself in the dining room; the first room I should have searched, hiding behind a huge vase of flowers, fiddling with the window latch. Moonlight filtered in, making me relatively easy to see if Fiona Tolliver came anywhere near, and I eased the window open, and had one leg in and one leg out, when the cat came in and made that dreadful noise again – like a wailing child. I had to get out, but my pyjama silk caught on a nail on the window frame, and I let out a yelp. I was about to climb out, as quietly as I could, when I heard the woman calling for her cat and, as I glanced towards the door, I saw the file – its edge, peeking out from beneath a bamboo mat on the table, pinned down by a vase.

I ducked back in, slid the file free, shoved it down the back of my pyjama trousers, and threw myself out of the window. It wasn't the elegant exit my entry into her house had been, and if it hadn't been for the cat leaping away from the frame and yowling loudly, I would have had no cover at all.

I heard Fiona's voice ring out again from the window, as I cowered in the trees' shadows. It seemed I'd been mistaken for a tomcat, but I stood where I was, still and quiet, as long as the window was open – and the woman gazed out of it for a full five minutes, under the light of the moon, and the driving rain.

Forty-Four

My late night out, resulted in a long lie-in, and I lay in bed, enjoying the rustle of leaves at the window – and the sound of someone coming up my stairs. And it definitely wasn't a dog.

'Oh! Maude!' I said, 'You gave me quite a fright.'

'A fright, at half ten in the morning,' she remarked, 'Is not a fright. It's a guilty conscience.'

'Yes, well, I got back a little later than I'd anticipated.'

'And you have a visitor,' she said. 'I thought I'd walk over with Mrs Tolliver, rather than let her in and have her get you up!'

'Fiona Tolliver!' I said, 'Well, that is a surprise.' I jumped out of bed.

'Tea will be ready in two minutes. I'll make a pot and I'll be leaving it in the kitchen – along with your guest.'

By the time I'd got up and pulled on a dressing gown, shoved the file in a satchel and kicked it – and the black pyjamas under the bed, Maude had gone, and the tea had been poured.

'Good morning!' said Mrs Tolliver, in a voice that sounded as annoyed as one would expect it to.

'What a pleasant surprise,' I said, reaching for my cup and raising it to my lips, when a small voice at the back of my head, asked me whether that was a good idea. If she was happy to steal people's writing, perhaps she was happy to administer poison. Perhaps Bettina had, unwittingly, uncovered something about the woman that implicated her in the murder of Old Cullimore, and written it into her story. (Had I solved two crimes in one go?) I kept my lips shut tight, and put the cup down, hoping what I'd just done hadn't been as obvious as it had appeared. I wiped my mouth with a handkerchief, and glanced down at it, to see if the lace had dissolved; wondering whether my mouth had turned blue yet. No, it seemed I was fine. Mrs Tolliver was drinking her tea very comfortably, but then, she would, wouldn't she?

I ventured to ask her the reason for her visit and, when she'd taken another generous sip of her tea, Mrs Tolliver told me that she'd missed me last night – when I'd come over.

'I... ' (What does one say to something like that?)

'You left one of your earrings behind,' she said, passing me a flower of pearls. My hands flew to my lobes, and one of them was bare. Dammit! Why had I worn such distinctive jewellery? (And damn those florals, too!)

'And I think you have something of mine,' she said in that small voice of hers; small, but very sure of itself. Something of hers? But the manuscript belonged to Bettina!

'I'm not sure I do,' I said in my most reasonable voice.

'Perhaps we should agree to disagree,' she said, primly, 'But you still shouldn't have been in my home.'

'Actually... actually, I was there to talk to you about something.'

'You were?' she said, and it seemed I might make an excuse for myself – if only I could come up with something. (Think Georgie, think!)

'Yes, I arrived and your door was ajar, there was no one home an-'

'I was at a bridge evening with your aunt,' said the woman.

'That may be so, but as you can see, we live separately and my aunt's social life is her own business. I arrived, there was no answer at the door, but it was ajar and I could hear sounds of distress. Like a crying child.'

She looked puzzled, until realisation dawned. 'That may have been my cat. It's a Siamese, they all sound like that.'

'That may be so, but it sounded odd, so, I decided to go inside to – to save the creature in distress, and that was when I noticed the file on the dining table.'

'On the dining table?' she asked, looking puzzled.

'Yes,' I said, with as much conviction as I could muster.

Mrs Stewart took a deep breath – and then seemed to deflate as she slowly let it out. 'It wasn't mine to read, but... I had to know what was in it. Certain people will profit from it who shouldn't, and certain *other* people will be ignored, their hard work withering on the vine and not recognised for what it was. Years of toil!'

Bettina's manuscript obviously covered a lot more ground than I'd imagined, and I hadn't expected a woman like Mrs Tolliver to be so keen to be involved in workers' rights.

'I'm sure that if you feel that strongly about it you could be added in,' I said, gently.

'It isn't me I'm interested in. It's a friend of mine. And it's too late now, surely?'

'Well –'

'Oh, of course, it's too late!' she said, suddenly cross at the thought – at my suggestion. 'And that's why I had to have it – to see what it said!'

'But you know it isn't yours to have,' I said, gently. 'It took a long time to write, and –'

'These things are the work of moments!' she hissed, 'A thoroughly thoughtless five minutes, and if it had been done properly, well, things could have been much better resolved!'

'Minutes!' I said, 'You've no idea how long these things take to create, and as for being done properly...' I said, although in actual fact, having never read any of my aunt's publications, I had no idea how well edited they were.

'A reputation ruined, years of care and all of it made a laughing stock with the stroke of a pen.' She wiped a tear from her cheek, and I didn't think it would be helpful for me to point out that Bettina used a typewriter, but she seemed to have calmed down.

Mrs Tolliver rose to leave the room and, when she reached the door, she turned, and quietly informed me that she would be telling the police about my walk-about in the house.

'But you're as much in the wrong as I am!' I said, 'I may have entered a property that I hadn't strictly speaking been invited into, but it was to retrieve a stolen file!'

My argument seemed to have worked. 'And much good may it do you!' she said, and Mrs Tolliver turned on her heel and left the room.

I wondered what exactly Bettina had written that could have had that effect on the woman – on a member of my aunt's fan club, and I took a sip of tea, before remembering that Mrs Tolliver may have poisoned it. Oh well.

Forty-Five

I had just finished dressing for elevenses (after a long, steamy bath in which to consider my findings of the last twenty-four hours) when I heard the sound of crunching gravel, looked out and saw a car drive by and park outside the front steps of the main house. It was a car I recognised by description only and, if what I'd heard about it were true, it was a miracle that it made it all the way up the drive. Mrs Stewart had come for a visit, driving her Austin.

She'd brought a bunch of flowers, and I hurried out to intercept her before she made it inside.

'Excuse me! Excuse me, Mrs Stewart!' I called.

As the woman turned, she had the good grace to blush beetroot red, but she managed a cheery "Halloo!" all the same. 'There you are! I was just looking for you. Your aunt told me you were in the cottage, and she'd said it was a bit gloomy, so I thought I'd bring you some flowers. I like to take flowers to all of my friends,' she said.

'Friends?' I said, and I recalled where I'd seen these same flowers before. At Mrs Tolliver's house the night before – and growing outside the library. They were little more than local weeds, and didn't compare with the bunch of flowers that Anthony had left in her porch.

'These are particularly difficult to cultivate and a local favourite,' she insisted.

'Depends on how often you visit the library.'

'Indeed,' she said, with furrowed brows, 'But these were grown specially. One shouldn't just *take* them!'

'There are a lot of things one shouldn't do,' I said, 'And one of those things is mowing people down in a great big car.'

'I don't know what you mean,' she said, meekly.

'You tried to run me down in that car you borrowed from the garage!' I cried.

Her lips trembled. 'I didn't mean to run you off the road! It was the Duchess! I just – I was driving down the hill, my shoe strap caught, and all of a sudden I couldn't brake – until suddenly I could.'

'And I was the one bumped, and sent hurtling across lanes of traffic!'

'Yes, yes, you were,' she said, red-faced.

'*And* I was bleeding from a head wound,' I said, but my anger had dissipated. She looked so forlorn I had to believe her, but I also had to ask, 'Why did you follow me to Breakwater?'

'I didn't,' she said.

'You did!'

'I wasn't there to see you. I was there to see – to check on one of the women there and I... well, time ran out. Visiting hours were over and so I left, and ran into you.'

'Was it Loretta you were there to see?'

'Be sure to put those flowers in water!' she said – as if she hadn't even heard my question – before jumping in her rickety old Austen, and driving off. If she'd followed me from the hospital in that car, she would have been the one in the ditch.

I went back to the cottage, dumped the flowers in the sink, and caught up with my aunt for lunch. She wanted to know how my investigation was going, and we discussed how the free-for-all atmosphere of the billiard room would have made it relatively easy to take a tray from one of the waiting staff, slip something into a glass, and pass it round, although the trick was ensuring that the person you wanted to poison, was the one who got the tampered-with drink. It was difficult to imagine how it could have been done.

'Difficult, but not impossible,' said my aunt, looking out of the window. 'If it stays dry this afternoon,' she said, 'I've a bowls match, so I'm afraid I shall have to leave you to work it out on your own.'

But I wasn't on my own.

I rounded up the writers and suggested a little drinks afternoon, and they were all so keen to be distracted, I could only assume they had strict deadlines they had to meet. I told them I'd invented a number of new cocktails and wanted to try them out for an article I was writing.

'Are you back on the magazine?' asked Lettice.

'No, I'm just writing something to send as a little reminder,' I said. 'I applied a while ago and haven't heard anything back, so I thought I'd tempt them with 500 words on "Your Room at the Ritz: Dazzling cocktails to Drum up at Home!"

'How about, "Hooch for Hubby"?' said Jack.

'We're not talking about moonshine here,' I said.

'Or "Mixing it up for your Man?' said Bettina.

'Mm, better.'

'"Cheers, My Dears!" is snappy!' said Jack.

'Oh, I like that!'

'Or you could write something awfully romantic,' said Lettice. 'You could make a little love story to go with each drink and you could call it "Cocktails", only instead of spelling the word with t-a-i-l-s at the end, you could spell it t-a-l-e-s! You know, like a story!' I thanked her for her suggestion.

The drinks recipes I'd drummed up, had actually come from the pages of my old magazine, and been written by my old colleague, Julian. And what was the point of this little get-together? To see if I could "poison my victim" each time I brought out a tray of drinks. However much I tried, Lettice would not take the drink I proffered, and always seemed to reach for the one at the back, the one at the side and, when I changed tack, the one right at the front. An hour after we'd started, the ladies were feeling the worse for wear (and each of them had voted for a different drink as their favourite).

I poured myself a "Love Potion", and a "Love at First Sight", mixed them together, and sank into an armchair.

Lettice asked me how my investigation was going, and I told her that I had the when, and too many why's and who's, so I had gone back to concentrating on the how's, but that it wasn't really working out. I also told her that I'd spent the last hour trying to poison her – which she took very well, considering. And that was when she dropped a little bombshell.

'Well, of course, there was no question of someone having poisoned Mr Cullimore's drink. He didn't take a single glass of anything all evening.'

'He didn't?'

'No. He was drinking from his hip flasks all night.'

'What?'

'He had one in each pocket. He said they contained scrumpy from one of his farms, although why anyone would drink that when champagne was on offer, is anyone's guess. He took every drink he was given, and passed them all to me.'

If Old Cullimore had been drinking his own rough cider all evening, how had he been poisoned?

'Um, Lettice, what did he eat?'

'Oh, I don't recall,' she said, which wasn't surprising given how much she'd drunk.

'All right, in that case, can you remember what *you* ate?'

'Before the ball, I had a cheese and pickle sandwich.'

'Yes.'

'Then I had a bowl of trifle when that came out, when I was dancing with Patrick Montacute.'

'*While* you were dancing with him?'

'Yes. Then I joined all the others in the billiard room, and there was no end of nibbles.'

'Was there anything that sticks in your mind?'

'The mini fruit tart thingies were nice. Those little sausages on sticks were also very nice, and of course the pineapple and cheese. That's my favourite.'

I couldn't help noticing that Lettice had gone with the options that Cook had thought up, rather than the more sophisticated fare made by the French chef my aunt had brought in for the evening, but then she surprised me by saying how much she'd enjoyed the vol-au-vent she'd had.

'Oh, and I was offered an asparagus roll – and everyone knows I don't eat anything green, but when Mr Cullimore saw the face I pulled, he was kind enough to eat it for me. He said it was his favourite thing, and that he grows the stuff.'

'Asparagus? I don't recall any asparagus.'

'There was only one plate of it, and you made such a fuss about it, Lettice,' said Bettina.

'There were *two* servings, and I didn't have either,' she pointed out.

'And who was it who offered the second plate to you?' I asked.

'Now, let me think, it was... either Elizabeth, Effie, Honey –'

'You mean Honoria?'

'- Amelia, Dilys or Fiona,' she said, taking a last swig of her "Love Conquers All".

'That's... that's the entire fan club, Lettice!' I said. 'And would *you* take any food from Effie?' I asked, remembering the state of her cottage.

'Any one of them could have given him some dodgy asparagus.' Bettina spoke in a tone that suggested that she was proud and pleased to have such a following. 'And don't forget Freddy,' she said, finishing off her drink.

'He's a funny old stick,' said Jack.

'Being a "funny old stick" isn't reason enough to accuse someone of murder,' I said, 'And if it were, half of Ampney would have finished the other half off by now!'

'Dilys is very good at mixing things,' said Jack, 'Have you tried her drinks? They're lethal!'

'Mm, perhaps they are,' I said. 'But, given that Lettice was drinking all Cullimore's drinks, I suspect the asparagus is the key. What about Amelia? Fiona?'

'Tolliver reminds me of an old school mistress I used to have,' said Lettice, with a hiccup.

'Well, I wouldn't trust any of them,' said Bettina, popping a cocktail cherry in her mouth.

Forty-Six

The rain that had not been forecast arrived as Maude came in with a large pot of tea and a plate of flapjacks, and my aunt returned home five minutes later.

I told her that my little experiment had been fruitless, and I broke the news to her about her fan club.

'But these women are bridge players and readers – not murderers!'

'I hope you're right,' I said, 'But at the moment, it's not looking good.'

'But what possible motive could any of them have?' asked my aunt. 'If only we had Old Cullimore's will. Mr Stone wouldn't have allowed it to go missing like that. Mr Tolliver has a lot to answer for!'

'Oh! Speaking of things that are missing -' I said, and I ran off to the cottage, and returned minutes later, half-soaked, with a satchel under my arm and a grin on my face. 'I've tracked down the missing manuscript!'

Where I would have expected a joyful clap of hands and expressions of gratitude and relief from my aunt and her ladies, I was greeted only with confusion. It was odd. 'The stolen manuscript!' I said, 'Bettina's work – I found it.'

'But where?' asked my aunt, with a face that wouldn't have looked out of place after an unsuccessful afternoon at the races.

'In Mrs Tolliver's cottage, on her desk!' I laid the satchel on the table. 'I was over there in an... investigative capacity.' Fortunately, nobody asked exactly what that meant, and besides, all eyes were on the satchel, as I opened its leather flap. 'Anyway... perhaps I'm too trusting, Aunt Sheba, but it never crossed my mind that a member of your fan club might have stolen it. Most of them were so keen to get their hands on it!'

'Well... that's good to know,' said my aunt.

'Am I permitted to look at the first page?' I asked.

'By all means,' she said, looking every bit as interested as I was.

So, I opened the file, only to find *The Last Will & Testament* of a Mr Francis William Cullimore.

Oh. That explained the file's flimsiness, at least. And the lack of Bettina's initials on the front.

'Well,' said my aunt. 'Where Mr Tolliver failed, you seem to have succeeded. Where did you say you found this?'

'Fiona Tolliver's house.'

My aunt raised her eyebrows in a questioning manner.

'Her desk,' I admitted.

'In the house of the solicitor's sister... And what did you say you were doing there?'

'I paid her a visit last night, after I saw her sneak out of her brother's office with the file under her arm.' (There was nothing to be gained by using the expression "broke in".)

'You paid her a visit, uninvited?' she asked, with a smile. 'Very interesting!'

'What does it say? What does it say?' asked Lettice.

'The question isn't what it says, Lettice, so much as what it says in comparison with the previous one,' I said. 'And that Last Will & Testament, I do not have.'

'But we know the previous one,' said my aunt. 'Henry managed to get his hands on it, copied it out and Mr Stone made some notes for me. He IS a useful man.'

Lettice sighed in a most un-Lettice like way, and my aunt went on, undeterred. 'And something -'

'Wait a minute!' I said, 'Who is this "Henry" when he's at home?'

'He's a useful sort,' said Jack, 'Lives locally, does a little work for Mr Stone, and he's Baxter's nephew.'

I turned to my aunt. 'But the way you spoke about him I thought he was a boy!'

'He is – he's about your age,' she said. 'Now, one thing Mr Stone was very keen to point out in his notes, was that a will in the possession of a solicitor does not mean that it was drawn up by a solicitor. As in this case.' She flicked to the second page, where we noticed that the witnesses were Justice of the Peace, John Parker (Dilys' husband) and my uncle.

'Lawrence, of all people, and he didn't say a thing!' said my aunt – and I was inclined to agree. Uncle Lawrence hadn't said anything pertinent when I'd grilled him at the Ritz.

We compared Henry's neatly hand-written copy with the document I had recovered from the solicitor's sister, and noticed that the same amount of money went to the gardener, the chef and his butler. And the amount stipulated in the earlier will, to be apportioned to his grandson and the sums equally apportioned to any great-grandchildren he might have, remained unchanged too, although obviously, in the newer will, that great-grandchild was named as Peter Cullimore. So, if either Peter or Anthony had killed their elderly relative, it hadn't been over money.

So, what was different?

'In the first will, Cullimore's nurse inherits five thousand pounds, and in his second will she inherits five thousand pounds. So, no change there, either,' said Jack.

'Except there is,' said Lettice – and we looked again.

'Oh,' I said. 'In the earlier one, the inheritance goes to "Nanny", and in the second, it goes to "Nursey". The first will was written shortly after his son, William died. He was doubtless, feeling rather mortal, and had decided to write a will. This second will was written very recently, and the nurse he refers to is Loretta Shields. So, who was the nanny?'

'It was Mrs Stewart,' said Maude, topping up the pot. 'She was like a mother to Anthony, by all accounts.'

Amelia Stewart had been dropped from Mr Cullimore's will – and she had tried to run me off the road, after following me to the nursing home, which could only mean that Loretta was in terrible trouble, and I only hoped we weren't too late.

While Jack called the police, to let them know that an officer should be sent to Breakwater Nursing Home, I wondered what evidence we had.

Mrs Stewart was one of three women who could have passed the fateful second serving of cyanide-sprinkled asparagus to Lettice, knowing it would be passed on to Mr Cullimore. Aside from a bunch of her flowers sitting on Mrs Tolliver's table, there was no evidence that she had actually seen the contents of the damning second will. And I had no evidence that Amelia Stewart had driven the garage's car with a view to running me down, after she'd followed me to see Loretta. Was Mrs Stewart behind the threats Loretta had received?

Unless some evidence was found to convict Mrs Stewart, she would get away with murder and, unless she was watched very closely, she could have a go at another one.

I suddenly felt very tired, feeling the effects of that last "Love at First Sight" with the ladies, and the rainy night I'd spent skulking about in a pair of pyjamas. Jack assured me that everything was being done that should be done, and I remembered that I'd left Crumpet alone for far too long.

I wandered back to the cottage, and was relieved to see the little dog in her basket, with a curt little note on the table, written by Maude, telling me to thank Baxter for taking her for a walk. I gave Crummy a dog biscuit, and put the kettle on for a pot of tea, and found a biscuit for myself. Maude hadn't touched the flowers in the sink though so, with nothing better to do, I got a jug off the top shelf, filled it with water, cut the stems and arranged the modest bunch. They were covered all over in some sort of pollen and didn't smell as nice as I'd expected, bu-

Forty-Seven

It was Crumpet who raised the alarm.

As is the way with her breed, she burrowed out of the cottage via a hole she must have been working on for some time, and barked furiously until Maude came out to investigate. I was taken straight to Doctor Ferguson in the Sunbeam, with Jack at the wheel, and within an hour of being found, I was back from the brink, conscious and eating ice cream in a bed at the cottage hospital in the centre of Ampney (the one I hadn't been allowed in before, because I wasn't an emergency).

'What happened, Georgie?' asked Jack. 'You gave us quite a turn.' My memories were hazy and, while I was giving it some thought, a nurse opened the curtain around my bed, and presented me with a large bouquet of flowers.

'Here you are, something to take your mind off your sore throat,' she said.

'Who are they from?' I whispered.

'The card is addressed to you, but there's no sender. Perhaps you have a secret admirer! Although, perhaps not... They're not terribly special, are they?' she said, brightly. 'One of our volunteers passed them to me, she might know. Nice lady – she used to work here. I could ask her, if you like?'

I managed to shake my head, which hurt, and I didn't need more conversation.

Still smiling, the nurse straightened my bedding and told me not to overexert myself, before opening the window for some fresh air. It was when the flowers shivered in the breeze, that I remembered the last thing I had done before collapsing. I wheezed to Jack to chuck the bouquet out of the window – which I'm pleased to say she did, *before* asking 'Why?'

'You see – WAIT – they're from Mrs Stewart – the old nurse – and they're covered in the evidence! Go down,' I croaked, 'Get the flowers back and DON'T give them a sniff!'

By the end of the afternoon, Mrs Stewart had been found; sitting half a mile from my ward, attempting to start her car. On the backseat was another bunch of flowers intended for Loretta, and liberally sprinkled with the same concoction of poisonous *pollen* as the two bunches I had been sent, and I realised that Mrs Stewart's former job as a matron, had prepared her for her life of criminal pharmacology. I was pleased to hear that Inspector Routledge had opened a file on her, and that the investigation into Cullimore's death was no longer considered to have been "by misadventure". The matter was out of my hands.

And I was even more pleased to hear that Routledge had bent Bettina's ear over my enquiries – and that she'd bent his ear in return!

I was released from hospital, two days later, and there was much gossip to catch up on, and so Lettice duly took a trip to the library to visit Mrs Burrows and make sure she was entirely up to date.

A couple of hours later, over a pot of tea and a slice or two of seed cake, Lettice told me that Loretta Shields was safe, and that she would be married to Peter Cullimore within three Sundays. Apparently, she hadn't been having an affair with Leo Adlington – a fact confirmed by Mrs Andrews, Ruby Parr and the vicar's wife, all three of whom kept rather a close eye on the man. She had been sitting for Leo, and the argument the two men had at the Art Festival concerned a marble bust of her that Leo had half-finished, which had been commissioned by Old Mr Cullimore and was less than half-paid for. And it was Leo who had waylaid Loretta in the Orangery, asking her to ask Old Cullimore about the money he was owed.

'And poor Fiona,' said Lettice. 'She's one of my biggest fans, and when she found out what Mrs Stewart had almost done to you – and what she managed to do to Old Cullimore, she told Inspector Routledge everything. She admitted to taking the old will from her brother's office – and then the new one, and showing them to Amelia. And with a little extra pressing, she admitted that Amelia had offered her a share of the spoils.'

'How was she able to find them when her brother wasn't?' I asked.

'She actually tried looking for them,' said Lettice. 'They were filed under 'O' for 'Old Cullimore.'

'Ah. What else did Mrs Burrows find out?'

'Mrs Stewart's finances were in trouble. Well, we all knew that, and it seems she wanted her share of Francis Cullimore's will sooner rather than later.'

'So, she hurried along his demise with a deadly asparagus canapé?' I asked. It was a vegetable she had known Lettice would avoid – and Amelia had evidently done a much better job of steering it in her direction, than I'd managed with those cocktails.

'And then, when she was given the more recent will by Fiona, she went in search of the woman who would benefit in her place,' said Lettice, shivering as she spoke.

'Loretta Shields.'

The question remained whether Amelia had known that Anthony, the little boy she had taken to Mrs Kibby's sweet shop, was to be a grandfather, courtesy of Loretta? I'd like to think she wouldn't have acted as she did, if she had known, but that wasn't for me to decide.

And what of Crumpet? The brave little dog who tunnelled out of the cottage and barked to save my bacon? She got some bacon. Good girl!

Forty-Eight

It was time for us to leave. The townhouse was "habitable", according to my aunt, and the writers were excited to be getting back to Pimlico. I, meanwhile, would be returning to my hovel in Clapham, and my paltry little wardrobe. Maude told me that my aunt's instructions were to "get a move on with my packing" (not Bathsheba's words, surely?) And I assured her it would take a matter of minutes, as most of what I owned was actually stuff that belonged to Crumpet.

Before we left, we gathered for a cup of tea. We would be driving in convoy, me driving the Sunbeam, with Crumpet, Crumpet's basket, a bag of Lettice's and a pile of Bettina's luggage, while Baxter drove the Bentley with Maude, my aunt, her cases – and the rest of Bettina's stuff. Jack had almost as little luggage as I did, which was just as well, because she was on her motorcycle. And Lettice and Bettina had already been taken to Kemble, to catch the 11.45 to Paddington.

The road trip would take three hours or so, depending on conditions; it was a breezy morning, and a ham sandwich and flask of tea on the way was all very well, but a quick cuppa before we left was always a good idea.

'Maude tells me you haven't packed,' said my aunt.

'I have! The Sunbeam is stuffed full,' I said.

'But she says the wardrobe in the Summer Bedroom hasn't been touched.'

'Louisa's clothes?'

'Of course! She doesn't want them back. Last season's cast-offs, the lot of them. You know what Loulou's like.'

'Oh, right – I – but, Auntie Sheba, that's wonderful!' The thought of returning to my sad little wardrobe of cotton, linen and cobwebs had been weighing on my mind in recent days, and I ran up the stairs before anyone saw the tears in my eyes.

I descended with armfuls of beautiful woolly, silky, suave and colourful clothing, which Maude wrapped in a sheet, and I folded and lay on the suitcases in the back seat of the Sunbeam. We were ready to go.

As I got into the front seat, my aunt told me she would see me in Pimlico, and I was grateful for the invitation to see them again before I headed south of the river. I didn't have anything else to do, after all.

We arrived before the writers, and my aunt and I had tea in a room she liked to call 'the Editor's Suite'. It was dry, and freshly painted, its Liberty print curtains had been washed, ironed and starched, there was cherry blossom on the branches outside, and the sky was a beautiful blue, without a single cloud in sight.

While Maude poured the tea, my aunt sat back in her armchair and regarded me. 'Georgie my dear, you've been here long enough to know a little about what we create, but you're probably wondering how our little publishing house is as profitable as it is?'

'I'm surprised it's profitable at all, seeing as I can't find any of your books. I have never seen one in a shop and I've looked all over.'

'Hm, well, in that case, you probably think our methods are a little strange?'

'Writers are all a bit odd though, aren't they?'

'That's as may be, but you see aside from our actual publishing – which is by subscription only, there's a little extra service we provide.'

'Oh, yes?'

'When we began, telephones were all the rage – well, of course, they still are – and I thought it would be just as well to enter our details into the directory, so I asked my secretary at the time to put them in. Whether it was her mistake, or the mistake of the person on the other end of the line, I don't know, but rather than our entry saying, "Love Lost & Found, Publishing Co.' It was printed as "A. Love, Lost & Found Property Co." And things have been a little unusual ever since. The following year, they corrected it, but still managed to leave the original in, and they've never bothered to change it.'

'So, what happened?'

'We were waiting to hear from aspiring writers, and from readers interested in signing up for our catalogue of books, but instead, we receive calls – we *received* calls – from people wanting to speak with Mr Love about their missing dogs, cats, parrots, handbags, husbands, wives and wedding rings. Things that they have lost – or found.'

'Annoying. And curious.'

'Annoying certainly that they think the owner of such a company must surely be a man, but that aside, it is curious, and fascinating too. People lose and find an awful lot of strange property – and they lose other people too, and a small number of the enquiries we have are simply too interesting to turn away.'

'I can imagine.'

'Now, I would just like to take this opportunity to make it quite clear that we are a publishing house, and our... *business...* is books,' said my aunt. 'It just so happens that, because of our directory listing – and through no fault of our own, we have the odd query that isn't of a literary nature, and is just too important to the person concerned, for us to turn our backs. And a lot of them become readers too!'

'You're finding things and writing at the same time?'

'Yes. Yes, we are.'

'But why don't these people go to – why don't you *send* them to the police station?'

'A lot of them have already been to the police station, and had no luck. And some of them don't want to, for whatever reason. And that's where you come in.'

'But I haven't lost anything – or found anything!'

'Georgiana, you have lost your husband, your career and your way. You find yourself with a new name, a married title and a little dog to look after, but I'm afraid you are at a loose end, with no job prospects in sight.'

I wasn't sure what to say; all the more so when she carried on.

'And you may not be able to help yourself, but helping others might go some way to sorting yourself out. And you never know, you might find another husband while you're at it. An unmarried one.'

'But -'

'Georgiana. You have been accused of murder, you've been to prison and you've got yourself out of it too, which is more than a lot of young people could have done, and then there was the business with Bettina's manuscript and Mr Cullimore. Added to which, you almost certainly saved the life of that barmaid friend of Peter's.'

'His wife-to-be,' I pointed out.

'Yes, well. All in all, I'm rather glad I didn't mention this little side-line of mine before the ball, otherwise I would probably have been added to your list of suspects.'

'Aunt Sheba, what do you mean?'

'The whole thing has been jolly useful as a kind of job interview, although murdering a man mysteriously so that my niece can find the killer, is a step too far,' she said. Seeing the expression of mild horror on my face, my aunt carried on. 'My staff helped to free you from Holloway, of course, but they were guided by what you discovered. And anyway, Bettina, Lettice and Jacqueline have writing to do. We're behind with the new season and it's time they rolled their sleeves up and applied themselves to their typewriters. So that is why I am offering you a job.'

'As a finder and returner of things?' I asked.

'Goodness no! As our resident travel writer and artistic editor, of course. No good reason for Lawrence to know that any of the income we make comes from an unlisted part of the business,' she said. 'We do need a travel editor of sorts, and besides, I suspect there's more to his statute-legislation-legal-parliament-whatever publishing house that he runs than meets the eye. I mean, there must be! Why does the government want accounts of what the government's doing? Shouldn't they already know?'

Forty-Nine

So, this strange little publishing house of Auntie Bathsheba's was making a pretty penny on the side, as a lost and found agency of sorts. And when my aunt let slip that the staff trip to the spa at Estoril the year before had been bankrolled by the money brought in by grateful patrons of *A. Love Lost & Found Property Company*, I began to see why she might want to keep it going.

My aunt must have interpreted my silence as trepidation, a lack of interest or doubt, because she went on to tell me that *Domestic Bliss,* the magazine for young wives that I had been writing for before my wedding – and subsequent imprisonment, was NOT interested in having me back. She'd had a word with the editor. Apparently, ex-cons were not in vogue this season.

'And when you say that I'd be your resident travel writer... editor...?'

'Well, what I mean to say is that you'll do some research work for the Girls. Lettice's Regency readers are very hot on their countryside settings, for example. You get the number of peals at St John's wrong and they'll let you know about it, believe me! The occasional trip to Cheltenham, Bath or the Peak District might be on the cards. And you'll have to write the odd essay whilst on your travels, wherever that may be, and they'll be collected up and published in some form or other in order to keep the Inland Revenue department happy. No point in puzzling the tax man.'

'And you've never considered doing this legitimately?'

'My publishing house has to do better than Lawrence's. His lot went to Biarritz last summer, and I will not be outdone.' She took a sip of her tea, and a deep breath. 'We want you for your travel writing and for assistance with the creative direction of our covers, and anyone who says different is telling fibs. And with Henry on board as well -'

'Henry? Henry, who?'

'Henry who found Cullimore's other will! I'm sure I've told you about him,' she said. 'He is an Ampney local but I think you'll find him quite useful. Now and again, a man is just the thing, and he assures me he has been to the city. You're to meet him tomorrow morning, Georgie, and you never know, if the two of you do well, we may manage *two* little holidays per year! Now, you won't forget, will you?'

Much as I wanted to know about this new colleague that my aunt was so keen that I meet, I was anxious to ask her one more thing before the ladies turned up.

I had broken into Mrs Tolliver's house to retrieve a document I believed to be Bettina's missing manuscript, and I couldn't shake the feeling that the writers' and my aunt's reaction to my finding Mr Cullimore's will – rather than Bettina's masterpiece – had been one of relief. And when I'd mentioned the (still) missing manuscript that morning at breakfast, my aunt had said, 'Oh, it'll turn up,' – as if it had been a mislaid stocking, or a pencil, when a couple of weeks earlier, she'd described it as "months of Bettina's best work". It didn't make sense. And so,

I suggested to my aunt that my first project should be to get to the bottom of the disappearance of Bettina's manuscript.

'Hm,' said my aunt, taking a loud slurp of Earl Grey.

'Or perhaps, Aunt Sheba, the question isn't so much who *took* the manuscript, as who *pretended* it had been taken?'

Silence.

'Is there something I should know?' I asked.

'There was a book published recently by that chappy, "D H" somebody – I never can remember his name. He wrote something about a stable boy and his mistress which caused a great hoo-hah, and although Bettina's been writing stuff like that for years, she's never got so much as a manacle around her wrist, let alone a writ. As far as I know, *you've* seen more action than she has.' I was about to say something, when my aunt must have seen the look on my face. She patted my hand. 'Of course, you were wrongfully imprisoned for the egregious murder of your new husband, and it had absolutely nothing to do with publishing laws or public decency. Quite a different matter. AND you managed to stay out of the papers, but we at *A. Love Lost & Found* wanted to make our mark, as it were.'

'So, did you lose it to promote it?' I asked.

'Something like that,' she said.

'Has it even been written, Aunt Sheba?'

'I believe Bettina has the bones of the thing and a list of names. And over the last couple of weeks, she has a pretty good idea of who really wants to be included in such a publication.'

'I can imagine,' I said. 'So, at the moment, it isn't so much "missing", as "imagined"?'

My aunt suddenly rose from her seat, and yelled, 'SHERRY, PLEASE!' – as Maude walked in with the decanter. 'And when Bettina does get around to writing it, I'll tell you who won't be included – Amelia Stewart! To think that I've played croquet with that woman. We've wielded mallets together on Chipping Wickbury Lawn.' She watched as Maude poured our drinks.

'Chin-chin, Auntie Sheba!'

'Absolutely. Well, it's always the quiet ones you have to keep an eye on,' she said, taking a sip and, as if to underline the point, she tripped over the coal scuttle and sent Xerxes and the aspidistra flying.

And that, dear reader, is how I got my job!

ACKNOWLEDGEMENTS

Thank you to the Oakeys, Clarks and Lawrences
for their enthusiasm, their encouragement
and their excellent spelling.

And thank you to Amanda, who is such a good story editor, and a super tea companion.

And to you, dear readers, thank you so much for your support.

If you enjoyed **"Death in Heels"**
please keep your eyes peeled for Georgiana's next adventure, **"Death in Tweed"**, and **"Death First Class"** (coming soon).

As always, I would be most grateful if you would leave a review wherever you buy your books. Authors really do love reviews almost as much as Crumpet loves a run around and a ham sandwich.

If you would like to know how Auntie Sheba met her ladies, pop along to my website, **eeoakeyauthor.com**, to sign up for

"Death Off Season"

It is a free-to-download novella – and very good fun.

And to find out more about me and Mrs Mortimer, we can be found on Instagram and FB, as **eeoakeyauthor**.

Printed in Great Britain
by Amazon

45607152R00148